What If ETs Are Real?

ALSO BY LG RICE

<u>**SECRETS OF SAGE MANOR BOOK SERIES**</u>

Through The Crystal Gate, Book One
Shadows Over Tanzlora, Book Two
Battle For Pisgah, Book Three

What If ETs Are Real?

L G Rice

Disclaimer:

This book is intended as a guide and exploration of the question: *What If ETs Are Real?* The information presented is based on the author's research, analysis, and interpretation, and it is summarized here for educational and informational purposes only.

All sources referenced throughout this book have been cited to the best of the author's ability. Readers are encouraged to consult these sources directly to gain deeper insight and draw their own conclusions. While every effort has been made to ensure accuracy, the author does not claim to provide definitive answers or guarantees regarding the topics discussed.

This book is meant to inspire curiosity, promote critical thinking, and serve as a starting point for further research into this fascinating subject.

To all my fellow humans who share my curiosity about the mysteries of the universe, this book is for you. May our collective wonder continue to fuel our journey toward discovery and understanding.

A Note to the Reader

Dear Reader,

This book is intended to serve as a guide and companion in your exploration of the profound question: *What If ETs Are Real?* It is not meant to provide all the answers but to spark your curiosity, encourage your own research, and expand your perspective.

At the end of each chapter, you will find a list of sources that I discovered during my research for my fantasy fiction novels, *The Secrets of Sage Manor*. These are invaluable resources that offer deeper insight and knowledge into the topic of if ETs exist. I encourage you to explore these sources and use them to dive further into this fascinating subject.

As I compiled this book, I realized that including every image, diagram, and document I discovered would make it impossibly thick and overwhelming. To keep this book manageable, I focused on presenting the key ideas and included all my sources so you can access the full breadth of information yourself.

My hope is that this book inspires you to question, explore, and imagine. Let it be the beginning—or continuation—of your journey into the mysteries of the universe.

With curiosity and wonder,
LG Rice

CONTENTS

Part I: The Cosmic Question

1

A Universe of Possibilities

Two possibilities exist: either we are alone in the Universe or we are not. Both are equally terrifying.
— Arthur C. Clarke

For centuries, humanity has gazed at the night sky, marveling at the infinite expanse of stars and wondering, *Are we alone?* This question, simple yet profound, has shaped human history and culture. It has driven scientific inquiry, inspired mythology, and fueled art and literature. Beyond its philosophical allure, however, lies an unsettling possibility: *What if extraterrestrial life is real, and what would that mean for us?*

To confront this question is to challenge deeply ingrained beliefs about our uniqueness in the universe. If intelligent extraterrestrial life exists, it would redefine humanity's place in the cosmos, forcing us to reevaluate everything from our religious doctrines to our scientific paradigms. For millennia, we have placed ourselves at the center of existence—first as the focal point of creation, later as the pinnacle of evolution. But the realization that intelligent life exists elsewhere would shatter this narrative, humbling us in the face of a vast, interconnected cosmos.

A Question as Old as Time

The question of extraterrestrial life is not a modern curiosity. Ancient civilizations pondered the possibility of beings beyond Earth. The Sumerians, for example, spoke of the *Anunnaki*, deities who descended from the heavens (Sitchin, 1976). Indian texts like the *Mahabharata* describe flying chariots called *vimanas*, potentially hinting at advanced technologies (Childress, 2013). Even the Greek philosopher Epicurus proposed that the universe contained "infinite worlds," many of which might harbor life (Rosen, 2012).

During the Renaissance, astronomers like Giordano Bruno advanced the idea that stars were suns like our own, surrounded by planets that could host life. Bruno's assertion, radical at the time, ultimately led to his execution in 1600. His ideas, however, laid the groundwork for modern astronomy (Martinez, 2018).

A Modern Obsession

The 20th century brought the question of extraterrestrial life into sharper focus. The advent of radio telescopes and space exploration made the search for alien life more tangible. In 1961, Dr. Frank Drake introduced the Drake Equation, a probabilistic formula to estimate the number of communicative civilizations in the Milky Way (Drake, 1965). Around the same time, UFO sightings and alleged alien encounters became cultural phenomena, fueling debates about government cover-ups and extraterrestrial visitations.

Hollywood played a crucial role in shaping public perception of extraterrestrials. Films like *Close Encounters of the Third Kind* (1977) and *E.T.* (1982) introduced the idea of peaceful alien visitors, while *War of the Worlds* (1953) and *Independence Day* (1996) portrayed extraterrestrials as existential threats. These narratives reflected humanity's ambivalence toward the unknown: Are we ready to embrace alien life, or do we fear its implications?

Cultural and Religious Significance

The possibility of extraterrestrial life touches every aspect of human culture. Religions, in particular, would face profound questions. Would the existence of aliens contradict sacred texts, or would it expand the understanding of divine creation? Some theologians argue that extraterrestrial life would not negate religious beliefs but rather affirm the infinite creativity of a higher power (Peters, 2014).

Philosophically, the discovery of intelligent extraterrestrial life would force humanity to confront its anthropocentrism. As Carl Sagan famously wrote:
"Our posturings, our imagined self-importance, the delusion that we have some privileged position in the universe, are challenged by this point of pale light." (*Pale Blue Dot*, 1994).

Why Now?

In recent years, scientific advancements have made the question of extraterrestrial life more urgent. NASA's Kepler and TESS missions have identified thousands of exoplanets, dozens of which lie in the "habitable zone" where conditions may support life (NASA Exoplanet Archive, 2023). Meanwhile, governments worldwide have begun declassifying reports on UFOs, now called Unidentified Aerial Phenomena (UAPs), lending credibility to sightings once dismissed as conspiracy theories (Cooper et al., 2017).

At the same time, new technologies like artificial intelligence and advanced telescopes have brought us closer than ever to detecting signs of life. As astronomer Sara Seager observes, "We are on the cusp of a new era in the search for life beyond Earth" (Seager, 2013).

Framing the Journey Ahead

In this book, we will explore the implications of a universe where extraterrestrial life is real. From ancient myths to modern science, we will trace the ways this question has shaped human thought and could define our future. We will examine the evidence, the theories, and the potential scenarios of contact, imagining a world where humanity takes its first steps into a larger cosmic community.

The night sky has always held mysteries beyond our comprehension. Perhaps it is time we stopped asking, *Are we alone?* and started preparing for the possibility that we are not. This is the journey of *What If ETs Are Real?*—a journey into the unknown, where every answer leads to deeper questions.

Sources

1. Childress, D. H. (2013). *Vimana: Aircraft of Ancient India & Atlantis*. Adventures Unlimited Press.
2. Cooper, H., Blumenthal, R., & Kean, L. (2017). "Glowing Auras and 'Black Money': The Pentagon's Mysterious UFO Program." *The New York Times*, December 16.
3. Drake, F. (1965). "The Drake Equation and the Search for Extraterrestrial Intelligence." *Physics Today*, 14(4).
4. Martinez, A. A. (2018). *Burned Alive: Giordano Bruno, Galileo and the Inquisition*. Reaktion Books.
5. NASA Exoplanet Archive. (2023). "Confirmed Exoplanets and Their Properties." Retrieved from exoplanets.nasa.gov.

6.   Peters, T. (2014). *UFOs—God's Chariots? Spirituality, Ancient Aliens, and Religious Yearnings in the Age of Extraterrestrials.* New Page Books.

7.   Rosen, R. (2012). *Epicurus and the Epicurean Tradition.* Cambridge University Press.

8.   Sagan, C. (1994). *Pale Blue Dot: A Vision of the Human Future in Space.* Random House.

9.   Seager, S. (2013). "Exoplanet Habitability and the Search for Life." *Proceedings of the National Academy of Sciences,* 110(48), 19273–19279.

10.   Sitchin, Z. (1976). *The 12th Planet.* Bear & Company.

2

The Vastness of Space

The universe is staggeringly immense—a seemingly endless expanse of galaxies, stars, and planets. To grasp the scale of the cosmos is to confront both awe and humility. Yet for much of human history, we have believed ourselves to be at the center of it all. The Copernican Revolution disabused us of that notion, yet some still cling to the idea that life, in all its complexity, exists only on Earth. But does that belief hold up when we consider the vastness of space?

The Cosmic Ocean

The observable universe spans approximately **93 billion light-years** across, a number so vast it defies comprehension (NASA, 2020). Within this expanse, there are an estimated **200 billion galaxies**, each containing hundreds of billions of stars (Hubble Space Telescope, 2020). And yet, this is only what we can observe. Beyond the edge of the observable universe lies a realm we cannot see or measure, where countless more galaxies may exist.

To put this in perspective: if every star were a grain of sand, the observable universe would be like all the beaches on Earth combined.

Around these stars orbit untold numbers of planets, some of which, scientists believe, may host conditions conducive to life.

The Goldilocks Zone

Not all stars are created equal, and not all planets are capable of supporting life. For a planet to harbor life as we know it, it must orbit its star within the **habitable zone**, often called the Goldilocks Zone—a region where conditions are "just right" for liquid water to exist. According to NASA, scientists have identified over **5,500 confirmed exoplanets** as of 2023, with many more candidates awaiting confirmation (NASA Exoplanet Archive, 2023).

Among these, dozens reside in their star's habitable zone. Planets like **Kepler-452b**, sometimes dubbed "Earth 2.0," remind us that our world may not be unique (Jenkins et al., 2015). But even this is a conservative estimate; the Milky Way alone could contain billions of Earth-like planets.

The Arrogance of Singularity

Despite this staggering abundance, humanity has often presumed its own singularity. Historically, this belief has been rooted in anthropocentrism, the idea that humans—and by extension, Earth—are the focal point of existence. This worldview was codified by ancient cosmologies and persisted through the Middle Ages, reinforced by theological interpretations of creation.

But as Carl Sagan famously observed, such a perspective reveals more about human ego than cosmic reality. In his seminal work *Pale Blue Dot*, Sagan writes:

"There is no hint that help will come from elsewhere to save us from ourselves. It is up to us. It's been said that astronomy is a humbling and char-

acter-building experience. There is perhaps no better demonstration of the folly of human conceits than this distant image of our tiny world." (Sagan, 1994).

It is, in fact, astonishingly arrogant to assume that in a universe containing trillions of planets, Earth is the only one to host intelligent life. Such a belief not only diminishes the potential richness of the cosmos but also blinds us to the broader possibilities of existence.

The Scale of Possibility

The sheer number of potentially habitable worlds suggests that life elsewhere is not just possible but likely. The **Drake Equation**, developed in 1961 by astronomer Frank Drake, attempts to quantify this likelihood. The equation factors in variables such as the rate of star formation, the fraction of stars with planets, and the number of planets that could support life. While the equation relies on assumptions, even conservative estimates suggest that there could be **millions** of intelligent civilizations in the Milky Way alone (Drake, 1965).

Humanity's Place in the Cosmos

If life exists elsewhere, it forces us to confront uncomfortable questions: What makes us unique? What responsibilities do we have as part of a larger galactic community? And, perhaps most troubling, why have we not yet encountered evidence of extraterrestrial civilizations? These questions drive scientific inquiry and speculative philosophy alike, reminding us of both our insignificance and our potential.

As we peer deeper into the cosmos, we must shed the arrogance that has historically defined our relationship with the universe. Instead, we should embrace the humility that comes with understanding our place in a vast, interconnected cosmic web. To think we are alone is to under-estimate the grandeur of creation—and the possibilities that lie beyond.

Looking Ahead

In the chapters to come, we will explore the scientific evidence and philosophical implications of extraterrestrial life. But one thing is al-ready clear: the universe is far too vast, too rich, and too full of possibil-ities for humanity to claim it as its own.

Sources

1.   NASA. (2020). "The Size and Scale of the Universe." Re-trieved from NASA.gov.
2.   Hubble Space Telescope. (2020). "Galaxies and the Expanding Universe." Retrieved from hubblesite.org.
3.   NASA Exoplanet Archive. (2023). "Confirmed Exoplanets and Their Properties." Retrieved from exoplanets.nasa.gov.
4.   Jenkins, J. M., et al. (2015). "Discovery and Validation of Ke-pler-452b." *Astronomical Journal*, 150(2).
5.   Sagan, C. (1994). *Pale Blue Dot: A Vision of the Human Fu-ture in Space*. Random House.
6.   Drake, F. (1965). "The Drake Equation and the Search for Ex-traterrestrial Intelligence." *Physics Today*, 14(4).

3

The Science of Life

Life as we know it depends on a delicate balance of conditions. But could life as we don't know it exist under completely different circumstances?
— Enrico Fermi

Life on Earth, in all its diversity, shares a common foundation: it is carbon-based, relies on water, and thrives within a relatively narrow range of environmental conditions. These shared characteristics have guided scientists in their search for life on other planets. But how universal are these requirements? Could alien life forms flourish under conditions we would find uninhabitable? Exploring these questions requires an understanding of the factors that make life possible—and the potential for life beyond Earth.

The Building Blocks of Life

All life on Earth is composed of six key elements: **carbon, hydrogen, nitrogen, oxygen, phosphorus, and sulfur (CHNOPS)**. Carbon, in particular, is crucial because of its unique ability to form complex, stable molecules. These molecules are the foundation of biological structures such as DNA, proteins, and cell membranes (Hazen, 2013).

Water, too, plays a critical role in life on Earth. As a solvent, it facilitates chemical reactions, transports nutrients, and helps regulate temperature. The presence of liquid water is therefore one of the primary criteria scientists use when evaluating the habitability of other planets (National Research Council, 2007).

However, recent discoveries suggest that life might not be limited to carbon and water. Some researchers have proposed alternative biochemistries, such as silicon-based life forms or organisms that use ammonia instead of water. While speculative, these ideas expand the scope of our search for extraterrestrial life (Benner, 2010).

The Habitable Zone

Planets capable of supporting life as we know it must exist in the **habitable zone** of their star, sometimes referred to as the "Goldilocks Zone." This is the region where temperatures are "just right" for liquid water to exist.

The distance of the habitable zone varies depending on the type of star. For example:

- Around smaller, cooler stars like red dwarfs, the habitable zone is much closer to the star.
- Around larger, hotter stars, it is farther away.

In addition to distance, other factors—such as a planet's atmosphere—play a critical role in maintaining stable temperatures. Earth's atmosphere, rich in greenhouse gases like carbon dioxide, helps trap heat and sustain a climate suitable for life (Kasting, 1993).

Extremophiles: Life Finds a Way

One of the most exciting revelations in modern biology is the discovery of **extremophiles**—organisms that thrive in conditions previously thought to be uninhabitable. These include:

- **Thermophiles**: Microbes that live in scalding hydrothermal vents, such as those at the bottom of Earth's oceans (Van Dover, 2000).
- **Halophiles**: Organisms that survive in environments with extremely high salt concentrations, such as the Dead Sea.
- **Acidophiles**: Life forms that thrive in highly acidic conditions, such as volcanic lakes.

The existence of extremophiles suggests that life could potentially exist in environments once deemed impossible, such as the icy moons of Jupiter and Saturn, or even the surface of Venus.

Potential Habitats Beyond Earth

Several celestial bodies within our solar system and beyond are considered candidates for hosting life:

1. **Mars**: Evidence of ancient riverbeds and the presence of subsurface ice suggest that Mars once had liquid water (ESA, 2022). Current missions like NASA's *Perseverance Rover* aim to uncover signs of past microbial life.
2. **Europa**: Jupiter's icy moon is believed to harbor a subsurface ocean beneath its frozen crust, potentially warmed by tidal heating (Pappalardo et al., 1999).
3. **Enceladus**: Saturn's moon has plumes of water vapor containing organic compounds, indicating the possibility of hydrothermal activity below its icy surface (Waite et al., 2006).

4.   **Titan**: Saturn's largest moon has lakes and rivers of liquid methane and ethane, raising the possibility of life with a non-water-based biochemistry (Hayes et al., 2008).

The Role of Star Systems and Galaxies

The type of star and its location within the galaxy also influence a planet's potential habitability.

- Stars that are too large and hot tend to have shorter lifespans, leaving little time for life to evolve.
- Galaxies contain regions where conditions are more favorable for life, such as the "galactic habitable zone," which has fewer catastrophic events like supernovae (Gonzalez et al., 2001).

Beyond the Goldilocks Zone

While the habitable zone concept has guided much of our search for life, it is increasingly clear that life may exist outside these constraints. For example:

- **Subsurface Oceans**: Bodies like Europa and Enceladus demonstrate that liquid water can exist below the surface, protected by ice and warmed by geothermal energy.
- **Atmospheric Life**: On Venus, where surface temperatures are extreme, scientists have hypothesized that microbial life might survive in the cooler upper atmosphere (Greaves et al., 2020).

These findings suggest that life may adapt to environments we have not yet considered.

The Implications of Discovery

Discovering life beyond Earth would fundamentally alter our understanding of biology. It would reveal whether life is a rare phenomenon or a common occurrence, shedding light on how life begins and evolves. If life exists in forms drastically different from those on Earth, it could expand the very definition of what it means to be alive.

But perhaps the most humbling realization would be this: if life is abundant in the universe, humanity's uniqueness lies not in its existence but in its awareness of that existence.

Sources

1. Benner, S. A. (2010). "Defining Life." *Astrobiology*, 10(10), 1021–1030.
2. European Space Agency (ESA). (2022). "Mars and the Search for Water." Retrieved from esa.int.
3. Gonzalez, G., Brownlee, D., & Ward, P. (2001). "The Galactic Habitable Zone." *Icarus*, 152(1), 185–200.
4. Greaves, J. S., et al. (2020). "Phosphine Gas in the Cloud Decks of Venus." *Nature Astronomy*, 5, 655–664.
5. Hayes, A. G., et al. (2008). "Hydrocarbon Lakes on Titan." *Nature*, 454, 607–610.
6. Kasting, J. F. (1993). "Earth's Early Atmosphere." *Science*, 259(5097), 920–926.
7. National Research Council. (2007). *The Limits of Organic Life in Planetary Systems*. National Academies Press.
8. Pappalardo, R. T., et al. (1999). "Europa's Subsurface Ocean." *Journal of Geophysical Research: Planets*, 104(E10), 24015–24055.
9. Van Dover, C. L. (2000). *The Ecology of Deep-Sea Hydrothermal Vents*. Princeton University Press.

10.   Waite, J. H., et al. (2006). "Organic Compounds in Enceladus's Plumes." *Science*, 311(5766), 1419–1422.

4

The Drake Equation

The universe is a pretty big place. If it's just us, seems like an awful waste of space.
— Carl Sagan

In 1961, Dr. Frank Drake, an American astrophysicist, introduced a groundbreaking equation to estimate the number of intelligent civilizations in our galaxy capable of communication. Known as the **Drake Equation**, this formula remains one of the most significant tools in the search for extraterrestrial intelligence (SETI). While its variables are speculative, the equation provides a framework for addressing the tantalizing question: *Are we alone in the universe?*

The Equation Itself

The Drake Equation is expressed as: $N = R^* \cdot f_p \cdot n_e \cdot f_l \cdot f_i \cdot f_c \cdot L$

Where:

- N = The number of civilizations in our galaxy capable of communication.
- R^* = The average rate of star formation in the galaxy.
- f_p = The fraction of stars that have planetary systems.
- n_e = The number of planets per star that could potentially support life.
- f_l = The fraction of those planets where life actually emerges.

- f_i = The fraction of life-bearing planets where intelligent life evolves.
- f_c = The fraction of intelligent civilizations that develop technologies detectable by us.
- L = The length of time these civilizations release detectable signals into space.

The values of these variables are still largely unknown, making the equation a thought experiment rather than a definitive calculation.

Breaking Down the Variables

1. **Star Formation Rate (R^*)**
   The Milky Way forms about **1–2 new stars per year** (Kennicutt & Evans, 2012). This value is relatively well understood due to advancements in astronomy and stellar observation.

2. **Fraction of Stars with Planets (f_p)**
   With the advent of missions like **Kepler** and **TESS**, scientists estimate that nearly **50–70% of stars** have planetary systems (Borucki et al., 2010). Exoplanet discoveries have confirmed that planets are a common feature of stars.

3. **Number of Potentially Habitable Planets per Star (n_e)**
   Among planetary systems, studies suggest that about **20% of stars host Earth-sized planets in their habitable zones** (Petigura et al., 2013).

4. **Fraction of Planets Where Life Emerges (f_l)**
   This remains one of the most speculative factors. While Earth provides a single data point where life has emerged, scientists debate whether this process is inevitable or exceedingly rare. Some

estimate fl could range from nearly **0 to 1**.

5. **Fraction of Planets Where Intelligence Develops (fi)**
Even if life emerges, intelligence might not. Dinosaurs thrived for millions of years without developing advanced technology. Estimates for fi vary widely, reflecting the complexity of evolutionary processes.

6. **Fraction of Civilizations That Are Detectable (fc)**
A civilization must develop technology capable of producing detectable signals, such as radio waves or lasers. Human technology has been detectable for about **100 years**, suggesting fc may be low for younger or less advanced civilizations (Shklovskii & Sagan, 1966).

7. **Longevity of Detectable Civilizations (L)**
The final variable is a reflection of how long civilizations last before collapsing or choosing to stop broadcasting signals. If L is short (e.g., a few hundred years), then the chances of overlapping with another civilization decrease. If L is long (e.g., thousands or millions of years), the likelihood of communication improves dramatically.

Applying the Equation

Using conservative estimates, the Drake Equation has been calculated to yield anywhere from **zero to millions** of detectable civilizations. Early optimistic estimates placed N in the thousands, while more conservative models suggest we may be alone—or nearly so.

For example:

- Optimistic scenario:

  ○ $R^*=1, fp=0.5, ne=1, fl=1, fi=0.1, fc=0.1, L=10,000$

Result: N=50

- Conservative scenario:

  ○ $R^*=1, fp=0.5, ne=0.2, fl=0.01, fi=0.01, fc=0.01, L=100$

Result: N=0.001

This range highlights the uncertainty and the importance of refining our understanding of each variable.

Criticisms and Limitations

1. **Speculative Nature**
   Critics argue that the equation relies heavily on assumptions. Variables such as fl and fi are difficult to estimate without more data.

2. **Anthropocentrism**
   The equation assumes life elsewhere would follow a similar path to that on Earth, potentially overlooking alternative biochemistries or forms of intelligence.

3. **Technological Limitations**
   We might not recognize alien signals or technologies, reducing fc in ways we cannot anticipate (Davies, 2010).

The Drake Equation's Legacy

Despite its limitations, the Drake Equation has been invaluable in shaping the search for extraterrestrial intelligence. It provides a framework for scientific inquiry, helping researchers prioritize targets and develop strategies for detecting alien civilizations.

Moreover, it forces humanity to confront existential questions: Are we special? Are we alone? And what does it mean to share the universe with others? As we refine our understanding of the cosmos, the Drake Equation serves as both a guide and a challenge to push the boundaries of human knowledge.

Sources

1. Borucki, W. J., et al. (2010). "Kepler Planet-Detection Mission: Introduction and First Results." *Science*, 327(5968), 977–980.

2. Davies, P. (2010). *The Eerie Silence: Renewing Our Search for Alien Intelligence*. Houghton Mifflin Harcourt.

3. Kennicutt, R. C., & Evans, N. J. (2012). "Star Formation in the Milky Way and Nearby Galaxies." *Annual Review of Astronomy and Astrophysics*, 50, 531–608.

4. Petigura, E. A., Howard, A. W., & Marcy, G. W. (2013). "Prevalence of Earth-size Planets Orbiting Sun-like Stars." *Proceedings of the National Academy of Sciences*, 110(48), 19273–19278.

5. Shklovskii, I. S., & Sagan, C. (1966). *Intelligent Life in the Universe*. Delta Books.

5

Fermi's Paradox

Where is everybody?
— Enrico Fermi

In 1950, during a casual lunchtime discussion at the Los Alamos National Laboratory, physicist Enrico Fermi posed a question that would later be known as **Fermi's Paradox**. The paradox arises from a simple observation: if the universe is vast, ancient, and full of stars with habitable planets, then intelligent extraterrestrial life should be abundant. So why haven't we encountered any evidence of it?

Fermi's Paradox is not just a question; it is a challenge to our assumptions about life, technology, and the cosmos. This chapter delves into the paradox, exploring the possible explanations for why we seem to be alone—or why we might not be.

The Vast Scale of the Universe

Fermi's Paradox is grounded in the staggering size and age of the universe. The Milky Way alone contains approximately **200 billion stars**, many of which host planets (Hubble Space Telescope, 2020). Based on the Drake Equation, even conservative estimates suggest there could be thousands, if not millions, of intelligent civilizations in our galaxy.

Additionally, the universe is **13.8 billion years old** (Planck Collaboration, 2018). With so much time and space, it seems statistically inevitable that intelligent life should have arisen elsewhere—and yet we've found no definitive evidence of it.

Possible Explanations for the Paradox

1. **We Are Alone**
    One unsettling possibility is that humanity truly is unique. Perhaps the conditions that led to life on Earth are so improbable that they have not occurred elsewhere. This explanation aligns with the **Rare Earth Hypothesis**, which argues that the combination of factors necessary for intelligent life—such as plate tectonics, a large moon, and a stable climate—may be exceedingly rare (Ward & Brownlee, 2000).

2. **Life Is Common, but Intelligence Is Rare**
    Life may exist elsewhere, but the evolution of intelligence capable of advanced technology might be exceedingly rare. Earth's history offers some support for this idea: for billions of years, life was limited to simple, single-celled organisms before the Cambrian Explosion 540 million years ago (Knoll, 2003). Even after complex life emerged, only one species—humans—developed the ability to create advanced technology.

3. **The Great Filter**
    The **Great Filter Hypothesis**, proposed by Robin Hanson (1998), suggests that there is a barrier preventing most life from reaching the stage of advanced technological civilizations. This filter could exist at any point in a civilization's development:

    *   It may be extremely rare for life to emerge at all.
    *   Intelligent life may frequently destroy itself through war, environmental collapse, or runaway technologies.

- Advanced civilizations may choose to avoid broadcasting their presence or exploring the galaxy.

4. **They Are Out There, but We Haven't Found Them Yet**
The simplest explanation may be that extraterrestrial civilizations exist, but we lack the capability to detect them. Our technology is relatively young—radio communication has only existed for about 100 years—and the vast distances between stars make detection challenging (Drake, 1965).

5. **They Are Avoiding Us**
Some theorists propose that advanced civilizations might intentionally avoid contact with less-developed species like humanity. This idea, sometimes called the **Zoo Hypothesis**, suggests that Earth is under observation, much like a nature reserve, and that intelligent extraterrestrials have chosen not to interfere with our development (Ball, 1973).

6. **They Are Already Here**
Another possibility is that extraterrestrials have already visited Earth but have chosen not to reveal themselves. Proponents of this idea often point to UFO sightings and alleged government cover-ups as potential evidence (Kean, 2010).

7. **We're Not Looking in the Right Way**
Finally, our search methods might be fundamentally flawed. Most SETI efforts focus on detecting radio signals, but alien civilizations might use entirely different forms of communication, such as laser pulses or quantum signals (Benford et al., 2010).

The Implications of the Paradox

Fermi's Paradox forces us to confront uncomfortable possibilities about the universe and our place within it. If we are alone, it raises profound philosophical and existential questions: Why us? What is our purpose in a silent cosmos?

Conversely, if intelligent life exists but chooses not to engage with us, it suggests a sobering reality about humanity's standing in the galactic order. Perhaps we are not yet ready to join a broader cosmic community—or perhaps that community has rules we cannot yet comprehend.

Looking Forward

As technology advances, so does our ability to search for answers to Fermi's Paradox. Missions like the **James Webb Space Telescope** and the continued efforts of SETI may one day detect biosignatures or technosignatures that confirm the existence of extraterrestrial life. Until then, Fermi's question—"Where is everybody?"—remains one of the greatest mysteries of the universe.

Sources

1. Ball, J. A. (1973). "The Zoo Hypothesis." *Icarus*, 19(3), 347–349.
2. Benford, J., Benford, G., & Benford, D. (2010). "Messaging with Cost-Optimized Interstellar Beacons." *Astrobiology*, 10(5), 491–498.
3. Drake, F. (1965). "The Drake Equation and the Search for Extraterrestrial Intelligence." *Physics Today*, 14(4).

4.   Hanson, R. (1998). "The Great Filter—Are We Almost Past It?" Retrieved from hanson.gmu.edu.

5.   Hubble Space Telescope. (2020). "Galaxies and the Expanding Universe." Retrieved from hubblesite.org.

6.   Kean, L. (2010). *UFOs: Generals, Pilots, and Government Officials Go on the Record*. Harmony Books.

7.   Knoll, A. H. (2003). *Life on a Young Planet: The First Three Billion Years of Evolution on Earth*. Princeton University Press.

8.   Planck Collaboration. (2018). "Planck 2018 Results. VI. Cosmological Parameters." *Astronomy & Astrophysics*, 641, A6.

9.   Ward, P., & Brownlee, D. (2000). *Rare Earth: Why Complex Life Is Uncommon in the Universe*. Springer-Verlag.

6

The Role of Exoplanets

> The discovery of exoplanets is one of the most profound achievements of modern astronomy. Each new world reminds us of the possibilities for life beyond Earth.
> — Sara Seager

The search for extraterrestrial life has taken a quantum leap forward with the discovery of **exoplanets**—planets that orbit stars beyond our solar system. In just a few decades, astronomers have identified thousands of these distant worlds, including many that lie in the so-called "habitable zone," where conditions might support life. This chapter explores how exoplanet discoveries are reshaping our understanding of the cosmos and fueling our search for life elsewhere.

The First Discovery: A New Era in Astronomy

The first confirmed exoplanet, **51 Pegasi b**, was discovered in 1995 by Michel Mayor and Didier Queloz, who were awarded the Nobel Prize in Physics in 2019 for their groundbreaking work (Mayor & Queloz, 1995). This planet, a "hot Jupiter," orbits its star at an incredibly close distance, demonstrating that planetary systems could be far more diverse than our own.

Since then, the pace of discovery has accelerated, thanks to advanced telescopes and missions like **Kepler**, **TESS**, and the recently launched

James Webb Space Telescope (NASA, 2023). These instruments have revolutionized our ability to detect and study exoplanets.

How Exoplanets Are Detected

Detecting exoplanets is a complex task, as they are much dimmer than the stars they orbit. Astronomers use several techniques to identify and characterize these distant worlds:

1.   **Transit Method**: By far the most successful method, it measures the slight dimming of a star as a planet passes in front of it. NASA's Kepler mission used this technique to discover more than 2,600 confirmed exoplanets (Borucki et al., 2010).

2.   **Radial Velocity Method**: This technique detects the wobble of a star caused by the gravitational pull of an orbiting planet. It was used to identify the first exoplanet, 51 Pegasi b.

3.   **Direct Imaging**: Although rare, this method captures actual images of exoplanets using advanced instruments to block the light from the host star.

4.   **Gravitational Microlensing**: This technique relies on the gravitational field of a foreground object to magnify the light of a distant star, revealing the presence of an orbiting planet.

Potentially Habitable Worlds

Among the thousands of exoplanets discovered, several stand out as potential candidates for life. These planets lie within their star's **habitable zone**, where conditions might allow liquid water to exist—a key ingredient for life as we know it.

1. **Kepler-452b**
    Often referred to as "Earth's cousin," this exoplanet orbits a star similar to the Sun and lies within its habitable zone. It is about 60% larger than Earth, with a similar orbital period, making it one of the most Earth-like planets discovered to date (Jenkins et al., 2015).

2. **Proxima Centauri b**
    Orbiting the closest star to our solar system, Proxima Centauri b is a rocky planet located in its star's habitable zone. However, its proximity to its star subjects it to high levels of radiation, complicating its habitability (Anglada-Escudé et al., 2016).

3. **TRAPPIST-1 System**
    This system contains seven Earth-sized planets, three of which lie within the habitable zone. The TRAPPIST-1 system is unique because all seven planets are close enough to study in detail using current and upcoming telescopes (Gillon et al., 2017).

4. **LHS 1140 b**
    A super-Earth located 41 light-years away, LHS 1140 b is a rocky planet with a dense atmosphere and a long lifespan, increasing its potential to host life (Dittmann et al., 2017).

The Importance of Atmospheres

The mere presence of a planet in the habitable zone does not guarantee its suitability for life. The planet's atmosphere plays a crucial role in determining its surface conditions. For example:

- **Earth's Atmosphere**: A balance of greenhouse gases like carbon dioxide traps enough heat to maintain liquid water without overheating.
- **Venus's Atmosphere**: Although Venus lies near the inner edge of the Sun's habitable zone, its thick atmosphere creates a runaway greenhouse effect, rendering it inhospitable.

Astronomers are now developing techniques to analyze the atmospheres of exoplanets, searching for **biosignatures** such as oxygen, methane, and water vapor. Missions like the James Webb Space Telescope will significantly advance this effort (Gardner et al., 2006).

Challenges and Limitations

Despite remarkable progress, the study of exoplanets faces significant challenges:

- **Distance**: Most exoplanets are located hundreds or thousands of light-years away, making direct study difficult.
- **Technological Limitations**: Current instruments can only detect certain types of planets, leaving many potentially habitable worlds undiscovered.
- **False Positives**: Biosignatures can sometimes be produced by non-biological processes, complicating the search for life.

Exoplanets and the Search for Life

The discovery of exoplanets has transformed the search for extraterrestrial life from speculation to science. Each new discovery adds to our understanding of planetary systems and the potential for life beyond Earth. As Sara Seager eloquently stated, *"We are on the brink of potentially finding life on another world. And for the first time in human history, we have the technology to do it."* (Seager, 2013).

Looking Ahead

In the coming decades, new missions and technologies will push the boundaries of exoplanet research. Projects like the **Nancy Grace Roman Space Telescope** and the proposed **LUVOIR Observatory** will allow scientists to image Earth-like planets directly and study their atmospheres in detail. With every discovery, the likelihood of finding a world like our own—and perhaps one that harbors life—grows ever greater.

Sources

1. Anglada-Escudé, G., et al. (2016). "A Terrestrial Planet Candidate in a Temperate Orbit around Proxima Centauri." *Nature*, 536(7617), 437–440.
2. Borucki, W. J., et al. (2010). "Kepler Planet-Detection Mission: Introduction and First Results." *Science*, 327(5968), 977–980.
3. Dittmann, J. A., et al. (2017). "A Temperate Rocky Super-Earth Transiting a Nearby Cool Star." *Nature*, 544(7650), 333–336.
4. Gardner, J. P., et al. (2006). "The James Webb Space Telescope." *Space Science Reviews*, 123(4), 485–606.
5. Gillon, M., et al. (2017). "Seven Temperate Terrestrial Planets around the Nearby Ultracool Dwarf Star TRAPPIST-1." *Nature*, 542(7642), 456–460.
6. Jenkins, J. M., et al. (2015). "Discovery and Validation of Kepler-452b." *Astronomical Journal*, 150(2).
7. Mayor, M., & Queloz, D. (1995). "A Jupiter-Mass Companion to a Solar-Type Star." *Nature*, 378(6555), 355–359.

8.   NASA. (2023). "Exoplanet Exploration." Retrieved from exoplanets.nasa.gov.

9.   Seager, S. (2013). "Exoplanet Habitability and the Search for Life." *Proceedings of the National Academy of Sciences*, 110(48), 19273–19279.

Astrobiology and Alien Life Forms

The universe is not only queerer than we suppose, but queerer than we can suppose.
— J.B.S. Haldane

Astrobiology, the study of life in the universe, seeks to answer one of humanity's oldest questions: *Are we alone?* While we have only one known example of life—Earth's biosphere—scientists have begun speculating about what alien biology might look like. Drawing from principles of biology, chemistry, and planetary science, astrobiology explores the conditions necessary for life and how it might evolve under entirely different circumstances. This chapter delves into the possibilities of alien life, from microbes to complex organisms, and the environments where they might thrive.

Defining Life

At its core, life is a system capable of growth, reproduction, and adaptation through evolution. On Earth, life depends on:

1. **Carbon-based chemistry**, due to carbon's versatility in forming complex molecules.

2. **Liquid water**, which serves as a solvent for biochemical reactions.

3. **An energy source**, such as sunlight, chemical reactions, or heat from geological activity (Benner, 2010).

However, these criteria may be Earth-centric. Alien life could challenge our definitions, prompting new ways of thinking about what it means to be alive.

The Building Blocks of Alien Life

1. **Carbon-Based Life**
    Carbon's ability to form stable, complex chains makes it the most likely basis for life. On Earth, carbon forms the backbone of DNA, proteins, and other essential molecules (Hazen, 2013).

    ◦ **Speculative Variation**: Alien life might also use carbon but rely on entirely different biochemistries, such as silicon-carbon hybrids.

2. **Alternative Biochemistries**
    While carbon is versatile, some scientists speculate that other elements could support life:

    ◦ **Silicon**: Silicon can form long chains similar to carbon, but its bonds are less stable in water. Silicon-based life might thrive in environments without water, such as Titan's methane lakes (Bains, 2004).

° **Ammonia**: Some have proposed ammonia as a solvent instead of water. It remains liquid at lower temperatures, potentially enabling life on cold worlds like Pluto or Enceladus (McKay, 1991).

3. **Chirality and Alien DNA**
Earth's life uses left-handed amino acids and right-handed sugars—a feature known as chirality. Alien life might have the opposite chirality, or even completely novel molecular structures, offering unique insights into the possibilities of biochemistry (Bonner, 1991).

Microbial Life: The Most Likely Alien Encounter

If alien life exists, it is most likely microbial. Microorganisms are resilient and capable of surviving extreme conditions, as evidenced by Earth's **extremophiles**:

- **Tardigrades**, which can endure the vacuum of space.
- Microbes found in hydrothermal vents, thriving in temperatures above 100°C (Van Dover, 2000).
- Organisms in subglacial lakes like Lake Vostok, which are isolated from the surface for millions of years (Priscu et al., 1999).

These examples suggest that alien microbes might thrive in environments ranging from Europa's subsurface oceans to Venus's upper atmosphere, where phosphine—a potential biosignature—has been detected (Greaves et al., 2020).

Complex Alien Life: What Might It Look Like?

While microbial life is more likely, imagining complex alien organisms reveals fascinating possibilities:

1. **Adaptations to Gravity**

    - On low-gravity worlds, organisms might evolve elongated limbs or lightweight structures.
    - On high-gravity planets, lifeforms might be squat and muscular to resist the force.

2. **Sensory Systems**
    Alien senses would likely depend on their environment:

    - On dark planets, organisms might rely on echolocation or infrared vision.
    - In methane-rich atmospheres, life might evolve chemical sensors to detect prey or mates.

3. **Energy Sources**

    - **Photosynthesis**: On planets orbiting dim stars, alien plants might appear black to absorb a wider range of light wavelengths (Cockell et al., 2000).

○ **Chemosynthesis**: Organisms in subsurface oceans, such as those on Europa, might derive energy from chemical reactions instead of sunlight.

4. **Mobility**

On gas giants, life might take the form of floating, balloon-like organisms buoyed by atmospheric currents, much like imagined in Carl Sagan's description of "floaters" in *Cosmos* (Sagan, 1980).

Speculative Life Beyond Chemistry

Some theories propose that alien life could be entirely non-biological:

1. **Plasma-Based Life**

In extreme environments like stars, plasma could organize into complex, self-sustaining structures capable of reproduction and adaptation (Tsytovich et al., 2007).

2. **Artificial Intelligence**

Advanced civilizations might transcend biology, creating self-replicating machines that explore the universe on their behalf (Tipler, 1980).

3. **Life in Higher Dimensions**

Some physicists have speculated that life could exist in dimensions beyond our own, imperceptible to human senses but influencing our universe in subtle ways (Kaku, 1994).

How Would We Recognize Alien Life?

Recognizing alien life depends on detecting biosignatures—indicators of biological activity. Potential biosignatures include:

- **Atmospheric gases**, such as oxygen, methane, or phosphine, in chemical disequilibrium.
- **Surface features**, like vegetation or thermal anomalies.
- **Radio signals** or other technosignatures from intelligent civilizations.

However, false positives are a significant challenge. For instance, methane can also be produced by geological processes, and oxygen might result from photodissociation in water-rich atmospheres (Catling et al., 2018).

Implications for Humanity

The discovery of alien life would revolutionize our understanding of biology and evolution. It could provide:

- **New insights into the origins of life**: Comparing Earth life to alien biologies could reveal universal principles and rare phenomena.
- **Technological advancements**: Studying alien lifeforms might lead to breakthroughs in medicine, energy, and materials science.

More profoundly, it would challenge humanity's self-perception, forcing us to rethink our place in the cosmos.

Looking Ahead

As missions like the James Webb Space Telescope and Europa Clipper search for biosignatures, humanity moves closer to answering one of the most profound questions: *What does life look like beyond Earth?* Whether microbial or complex, carbon-based or not, alien life will forever change the way we view the universe—and ourselves.

Sources

1.   Bains, W. (2004). "Many Chemistries Could Be Used to Build Living Systems." *Astrobiology*, 4(2), 137–167.
2.   Benner, S. A. (2010). "Defining Life." *Astrobiology*, 10(10), 1021–1030.
3.   Bonner, W. A. (1991). "The Origin and Amplification of Biomolecular Chirality." *Origins of Life and Evolution of the Biosphere*, 21(2), 59–111.
4.   Catling, D. C., et al. (2018). "Biosignatures and False Positives in Exoplanet Research." *Science Advances*, 4(8), eaau3074.
5.   Cockell, C. S., et al. (2000). "The Ultraviolet Environment of Earth-Like Planets Orbiting M Stars." *Icarus*, 146(2), 343–359.
6.   Greaves, J. S., et al. (2020). "Phosphine Gas in the Cloud Decks of Venus." *Nature Astronomy*, 5, 655–664.
7.   Hazen, R. M. (2013). *The Story of Earth: The First 4.5 Billion Years, from Stardust to Living Planet*. Viking.
8.   Kaku, M. (1994). *Hyperspace: A Scientific Odyssey through Parallel Universes, Time Warps, and the 10th Dimension*. Oxford University Press.

9.   McKay, C. P. (1991). "Planetary Atmospheres and the Search for Life." *Reviews of Geophysics*, 29(2), 200–204.

10.   Priscu, J. C., et al. (1999). "Geomicrobiology of Subglacial Ice Above Lake Vostok, Antarctica." *Science*, 286(5447), 2141–2144.

11.   Sagan, C. (1980). *Cosmos*. Random House.

12.   Tsytovich, V. N., et al. (2007). "From Plasma Crystals and Helical Structures towards Inorganic Living Matter." *New Journal of Physics*, 9(8), 263.

13.   Van Dover, C. L. (2000). *The Ecology of Deep-Sea Hydrothermal Vents*. Princeton University Press.

Part II: Evidence of the Unknown

8

Ancient Mysteries and ETs

> The truth is out there, hidden in plain sight, whispered
> in myths, carved in stone, and told through the stars.
> — Unknown

The idea that ancient civilizations may have had contact with extraterrestrials is a compelling theory that spans cultures and epochs. From the intricate carvings of the Mayan pyramids to the enigmatic construction of the Great Pyramid of Giza, proponents of the "ancient astronaut theory" suggest that advanced beings might have influenced human development. This chapter explores these possibilities, examining historical records, artifacts, and the controversial works of researchers like Dr. Tom Horn and Cris Putnam, although both are now deceased, their writings connect extraterrestrials, biblical prophecy, and the Vatican.

The Ancient Astronaut Theory

The ancient astronaut theory posits that extraterrestrials visited Earth in the distant past, interacting with early humans and influencing the development of civilizations. Proponents argue that myths, legends, and unexplained technological feats might reflect encounters with advanced beings.

Key examples include:

- **The Sumerian Anunnaki**: The Sumerians believed that the Anunnaki were gods who descended from the heavens to create and guide humanity (Sitchin, 1976). Some interpretations suggest these "gods" might have been extraterrestrials.
- **The Pyramids of Giza**: The precision of the Great Pyramid's construction has led some to speculate that advanced technology—or even extraterrestrial knowledge—played a role.
- **Nazca Lines**: These enormous geoglyphs in Peru are visible only from the air, fueling speculation that they were created as signals or markers for aerial visitors (von Däniken, 1968).

Cross-Cultural Evidence

1. **Indian Texts and Vimanas**
   Ancient Indian scriptures like the *Mahabharata* and *Ramayana* describe flying chariots called vimanas, which were capable of interstellar travel. These texts also reference advanced weaponry that some interpret as evidence of extraterrestrial technology (Childress, 2013).

2. **Dogon Tribe and Sirius**
   The Dogon tribe in Mali possesses advanced astronomical knowledge, including details about the Sirius star system, which they claim was given to them by beings from Sirius. This knowledge predates modern telescopic discovery, raising questions about its origins (Temple, 1998).

3. **Mesoamerican Cultures**
   Mayan and Aztec civilizations were advanced in astronomy and engineering. The Mayan calendar and their depiction of gods descending from the sky have been linked to extraterrestrial theories (von Däniken, 1970).

The Vatican's Connection to Extraterrestrial Theories

The works of the late Dr. Tom Horn and the late Cris Putnam delve into the Vatican's historical and theological perspectives on extraterrestrials. In *Exo-Vaticana: Petrus Romanus, Project Lucifer, and the Vatican's Astonishing Plan for the Arrival of an Alien Savior* (2013), Horn and Putnam explore how the Catholic Church has positioned itself to address the potential discovery of extraterrestrial life.

1. **The Vatican Observatory and Project LUCIFER**
   The Vatican Observatory's Advanced Technology Telescope (VATT), often linked to Project LUCIFER (Large Binocular Telescope Near-Infrared Utility with Camera and Integral Field Unit for Extragalactic Research), has fueled speculation about the Church's interest in studying celestial phenomena (Horn & Putnam, 2013).

   ◦ Horn and Putnam argue that the Vatican may anticipate extraterrestrial contact and its theological implications.

2. **The Wormwood Prophecies**
   In *The Wormwood Prophecy* (2019), the late Dr. Horn connects the biblical reference to "Wormwood" in Revelation 8:10–11 to a celestial object, potentially an asteroid or alien spacecraft, that could bring devastation to Earth. He suggested that extraterrestrial involvement could align with end-times prophecy.

3. **Statements from Vatican Officials**
   Prominent Vatican astronomers, such as Brother Guy Consolmagno, have made public statements suggesting that the discovery of extraterrestrial life would not contradict Christian theology. Consolmagno even stated that he would baptize an

alien if they asked, signaling the Church's openness to extraterrestrial possibilities (Consolmagno, 2014).

Interpreting Ancient Texts

Many religious texts contain descriptions that could be interpreted as encounters with extraterrestrials:

- **The Book of Ezekiel**: The prophet's vision of a "wheel within a wheel" has been interpreted by some as a description of a UFO.
- **The Nephilim**: In Genesis 6:4, the Nephilim are described as the offspring of "sons of God" and "daughters of men." Some theorists suggest this could refer to extraterrestrial beings mating with humans (Horn & Putnam, 2013).

Skepticism and Alternative Views

Critics argue that the ancient astronaut theory often overlooks more plausible explanations:

- Advances in archaeology and engineering have provided naturalistic explanations for many ancient mysteries.
- Claims of extraterrestrial influence often lack concrete evidence and rely on speculative interpretations of historical records (Shermer, 2002).

Despite this, the theory remains popular, as it offers an imaginative lens through which to view human history and achievements.

Implications of Extraterrestrial Involvement

If ancient civilizations were influenced by extraterrestrials, it raises profound questions:

- **Cultural and Technological Development**: How much of human progress can be attributed to extraterrestrial guidance?
- **Theological Implications**: Would such interactions challenge traditional religious doctrines or validate them?
- **Purpose of Contact**: Were extraterrestrials aiding humanity, observing us, or pursuing their own agenda?

Looking Ahead

The intersection of ancient mysteries and extraterrestrial theories continues to captivate the public imagination. While definitive proof remains elusive, ongoing research and discoveries may one day shed light on these tantalizing possibilities.

Sources

1. Childress, D. H. (2013). *Vimana: Aircraft of Ancient India & Atlantis*. Adventures Unlimited Press.
2. Consolmagno, G. (2014). *Would You Baptize an Extraterrestrial?*. Image.
3. Horn, T., & Putnam, C. (2013). *Exo-Vaticana: Petrus Romanus, Project Lucifer, and the Vatican's Astonishing Plan for the Arrival of an Alien Savior*. Defender Publishing.
4. Horn, T. (2019). *The Wormwood Prophecy*. Charisma House.
5. Shermer, M. (2002). *Why People Believe Weird Things: Pseudoscience, Superstition, and Other Confusions of Our Time*. Holt Paperbacks.
6. Sitchin, Z. (1976). *The 12th Planet*. Harper.

7.	Temple, R. (1998). *The Sirius Mystery*. Destiny Books.

8.	von Däniken, E. (1968). *Chariots of the Gods?*. Putnam.

9

The UFO Phenomenon

The phenomenon of UFOs does not present itself as something easy to define, explain, or dismiss. It is a subject that demands rigorous investigation and open-minded inquiry.
— Dr. Steven Greer

The UFO phenomenon has captivated public imagination and scientific curiosity for decades. What was once dismissed as fringe speculation has gained increasing legitimacy due to government disclosures, eyewitness testimony, and investigative research. This chapter explores the history of UFO sightings, evaluates their credibility, and highlights the research and published findings of notable figures such as Dr. Steven Greer and L.A. Marzulli, whose work bridges the gap between evidence and speculation.

A Brief History of UFO Sightings

1.   Early Sightings

Reports of unidentified flying objects date back centuries. Ancient texts and artwork often depict strange objects in the sky, interpreted by some as evidence of UFO activity. Examples include:

- The *Annales Laurissenses* (776 AD), which describes fiery globes hovering above a Saxon army.
- Medieval paintings, such as "The Madonna with Saint Giovannino," featuring unexplained aerial objects (Marzulli, 2017).

2. **The Modern Era of UFOs**

The UFO phenomenon gained significant attention in the 20th century, beginning with:

- **The Kenneth Arnold Sighting (1947)**: Pilot Kenneth Arnold reported seeing nine crescent-shaped objects flying at high speed near Mount Rainier. His description popularized the term "flying saucer."
- **Roswell Incident (1947)**: The alleged crash of an unidentified object in Roswell, New Mexico, remains one of the most famous UFO cases. Initial reports described the recovery of a "flying disc," though the U.S. military later claimed it was a weather balloon.

3. **Military Encounters**

- **Project Blue Book (1952–1969)**: The U.S. Air Force investigated over 12,000 UFO sightings, concluding that the majority were explainable but leaving a small percentage unexplained (Ruppelt, 1956).
- **The Tic Tac UFO (2004)**: U.S. Navy pilots recorded infrared footage of an object exhibiting flight characteristics far beyond known technology, reigniting debates

about the existence of advanced extraterrestrial craft (Fravor, 2020).

Credibility and Government Disclosures

1. **Declassified Reports**

   In recent years, governments have declassified previously secret UFO investigations:

   - **The Pentagon's UAP Report (2021)**: The Office of the Director of National Intelligence (ODNI) released a report analyzing 144 UAP (Unidentified Aerial Phenomena) incidents, with 143 remaining unexplained (ODNI, 2021).
   - **AATIP (2007–2012)**: The Advanced Aerospace Threat Identification Program studied UAP encounters, highlighting the potential security implications of unidentified aerial technology (Kean, 2017).

2. **Testimony from Military Personnel**

   Eyewitness accounts from credible sources, such as fighter pilots and radar operators, lend weight to UFO reports. Retired U.S. Navy Commander David Fravor described his 2004 encounter with a "Tic Tac" object as demonstrating "otherworldly" capabilities (Fravor, 2020).

Dr. Steven Greer's Contributions

Dr. Steven Greer, a prominent researcher and founder of the Disclosure Project, has spent decades investigating UFOs and advocating for transparency:

1. **The Disclosure Project (2001)**

   ○ Dr. Greer organized a press conference featuring testimony from military, intelligence, and government officials about their encounters with UFOs. Many witnesses described direct knowledge of UFO retrieval operations and alleged government cover-ups (Greer, 2001).

2. **Documentaries**

   ○ **Sirius (2013)**: This documentary explores UFO secrecy, featuring whistleblower testimony and the controversial examination of a six-inch humanoid skeleton (Greer, 2013).
   ○ **Unacknowledged (2017)**: Focused on government secrecy, this film highlights the potential implications of advanced extraterrestrial technology for humanity (Greer, 2017).
   ○ **Close Encounters of the Fifth Kind (2020)**: Greer introduces techniques for initiating contact with extraterrestrials, emphasizing the role of consciousness (Greer, 2020).

3. **Published Findings**

   Dr. Greer's book *Unacknowledged: An Exposé of the World's Greatest Secret* (2017) details decades of suppressed UFO research and argues for the societal benefits of revealing extraterrestrial technology.

L.A. Marzulli's Research

L.A. Marzulli focuses on the intersection of UFOs, biblical prophecy, and ancient history:

1. **Nephilim and UFOs**
   In his book series *The Nephilim Trilogy*, Marzulli connects the biblical Nephilim to UFO activity, suggesting that modern abductions and sightings may involve the same entities described in Genesis 6:4 (Marzulli, 2017).

2. **Documentaries**

   ◦ **The Watchers Series**: Marzulli's award-winning series explores topics such as alien implants, crop circles, and UFO sightings, often featuring firsthand accounts and expert analyses (Marzulli, 2013).
   ◦ **On the Trail of the Nephilim**: This investigative series examines ancient megalithic structures and their potential links to extraterrestrial influence (Marzulli, 2017).

3. **Implant Removal Studies**
   Marzulli has documented cases of individuals who claim to have alien implants, including surgical procedures to remove these objects. Analyses suggest the implants contain exotic materials not of earthly origin, though these claims remain controversial (Marzulli, 2017).

The UFO Phenomenon's Broader Implications

1. **Technological Insights**

   If UFOs represent advanced technology, studying them could revolutionize energy, propulsion, and transportation systems. Dr. Greer has argued that extraterrestrial technology could provide clean, limitless energy, solving global resource crises (Greer, 2017).

2. **Theological Questions**

   Marzulli's work raises profound theological questions: Are UFOs evidence of advanced civilizations, or could they represent spiritual entities with a role in humanity's history?

3. **Societal Impact**

   The confirmation of extraterrestrial life would challenge societal structures, forcing humanity to reevaluate its place in the universe and potentially uniting us in a shared cosmic perspective.

Looking Ahead

As governments release more information and researchers like Dr. Greer and L.A. Marzulli continue their investigations, the UFO phenomenon remains at the forefront of public interest. Whether these objects are extraterrestrial, interdimensional, or something else entirely, understanding their nature could unlock answers to some of humanity's greatest mysteries.

Sources

1. Fravor, D. (2020). Testimony in *The Phenomenon* documentary. James Fox, Director.

2.	Greer, S. (2001). *The Disclosure Project Briefing Document.*

3.	Greer, S. (2013). *Sirius* [Film].

4.	Greer, S. (2017). *Unacknowledged: An Exposé of the World's Greatest Secret.* A&M Publishing.

5.	Greer, S. (2020). *Close Encounters of the Fifth Kind* [Film].

6.	Kean, L. (2017). *UFOs: Generals, Pilots, and Government Officials Go on the Record.* Crown Publishing Group.

7.	Marzulli, L.A. (2013). *The Watchers Series* [Film Series]. Spiral of Life.

8.	Marzulli, L.A. (2017). *On the Trail of the Nephilim.* Spiral of Life.

9.	ODNI. (2021). "Preliminary Assessment: Unidentified Aerial Phenomena." Office of the Director of National Intelligence.

10.	Ruppelt, E. J. (1956). *The Report on Unidentified Flying Objects.* Doubleday.

10

The Roswell Incident

For many, the Roswell incident is the genesis of modern UFO conspiracy theories—a singular event that continues to fuel speculation about extraterrestrial life and government cover-ups.
— Anonymous

The Roswell incident, which took place in July 1947, remains one of the most enduring and controversial events in the history of UFO phenomena. What began as a report of a mysterious crash in the New Mexico desert quickly spiraled into a tale of secrecy, conspiracy, and alleged extraterrestrial involvement. This chapter revisits the Roswell incident, examining the evidence, official explanations, and the cultural legacy of the event that sparked modern UFO conspiracy theories.

The Events of July 1947

1. **Initial Reports**

   ○ On July 8, 1947, the Roswell Army Air Field (RAAF) issued a press release stating that they had recovered a "flying disc" from a ranch near Roswell, New Mexico. The announcement was reported in local newspapers, including the *Roswell Daily Record*, with the headline:

"RAAF Captures Flying Saucer on Ranch in Roswell Region" (*Roswell Daily Record*, 1947).

- Rancher Mac Brazel had discovered strange debris on his property days earlier, including metallic fragments and materials he described as lightweight yet unusually strong.

2. Official Retraction

- Just one day after the initial report, the U.S. Army Air Force issued a retraction, claiming the debris was from a weather balloon, not a "flying disc." Photographs were released showing military personnel with pieces of the alleged balloon, including Major Jesse Marcel, who later expressed doubts about the official explanation (Marcel, 1980).

Theories and Allegations

1. The Extraterrestrial Hypothesis

- Proponents of this theory argue that the debris recovered in Roswell was from an alien spacecraft, and that the U.S. government orchestrated a cover-up to conceal the discovery.
- Witnesses, including military personnel, have described materials with properties that defied known technology, such as "memory metal" that returned to its original shape after being crumpled (Randle, 1995).

2. Project Mogul

- In the 1990s, the U.S. Air Force declassified documents revealing that the Roswell debris was likely from **Project Mogul**, a top-secret program using high-altitude balloons to monitor Soviet nuclear tests (USAF, 1994).
- While this explanation aligns with the timing and nature of the debris, skeptics argue that it fails to account for eyewitness descriptions of unusual materials and the enduring secrecy surrounding the incident.

3. **Alien Bodies**

- Some accounts claim that alien bodies were recovered from the crash site. Glenn Dennis, a mortician in Roswell at the time, alleged that he received inquiries from the military about preserving non-human remains (Dennis & Carey, 1991).
- The **Alien Autopsy Film** released in 1995 purported to show the dissection of an extraterrestrial being recovered from Roswell, though it was later admitted to be a hoax.

Eyewitness Testimonies

1. **Major Jesse Marcel**

- Marcel, the intelligence officer who first investigated the debris, later stated that the materials were unlike anything he had seen before, describing them as extraordinarily light and strong (Marcel, 1980).

2. **Colonel Philip Corso**

  ◦ In his book *The Day After Roswell*, Corso claimed that he was involved in distributing recovered alien technology to private companies for reverse engineering, leading to advancements in fiber optics, microchips, and other technologies (Corso, 1997).

3. **Other Witnesses**

  ◦ Numerous civilians and military personnel have come forward over the years, providing varying accounts of the incident. Some describe threats and intimidation by government agents, while others report seeing unearthly materials or bodies.

The Cultural Impact of Roswell

1. **The Birth of UFO Conspiracy Theories**

  ◦ Roswell is widely regarded as the event that catalyzed modern UFO conspiracy theories. The incident introduced the idea of a government cover-up to the public consciousness, inspiring countless books, films, and documentaries.

2. **Roswell's Role in Pop Culture**

○   The Roswell story has been referenced in films like *Independence Day* (1996) and TV shows such as *The X-Files*. The town of Roswell has embraced its association with UFOs, hosting an annual UFO Festival and maintaining a UFO museum.

3.   **Skepticism and Debunking**

○   Critics argue that the Roswell story has been exaggerated over time, with elements such as alien bodies and advanced technology added through speculation and misinterpretation. While many believe the official Project Mogul explanation, others see it as part of an ongoing disinformation campaign.

The Legacy of Roswell

The Roswell incident remains unresolved, straddling the line between history and mythology. Whether it was a weather balloon, an alien spacecraft, or something else entirely, its significance lies in its enduring ability to provoke questions about government secrecy and the possibility of extraterrestrial life.

For believers, Roswell is proof of a cover-up that has hidden the truth about UFOs for decades. For skeptics, it is a cautionary tale about the power of speculation and the human tendency to find patterns in the unexplained. Either way, the legacy of Roswell ensures that the debate about UFOs and extraterrestrial life will continue for generations.

Sources

1.   Corso, P. (1997). *The Day After Roswell*. Pocket Books.
2.   Dennis, G., & Carey, S. (1991). *Witness to Roswell: Unmasking the 60-Year Cover-Up*. New Page Books.
3.   Marcel, J. (1980). Interview with *National Enquirer*.
4.   Randle, K. D. (1995). *The Roswell UFO Crash: What They Don't Want You to Know*. Avon Books.
5.   *Roswell Daily Record*. (1947). "RAAF Captures Flying Saucer on Ranch in Roswell Region."
6.   USAF. (1994). *The Roswell Report: Fact vs. Fiction in the New Mexico Desert*. U.S. Air Force.

11

Government Secrets and the Roswell Incident

It is no coincidence that UFO sightings increased dramatically during the era of nuclear testing. Could humanity's atomic experimentation have drawn the attention of extraterrestrial civilizations? — Anonymous

The Roswell incident is often regarded as a pivotal moment in UFO history, sparking modern conspiracy theories about extraterrestrial life and government cover-ups. While official explanations attribute the event to terrestrial causes, alternative theories suggest a deeper cosmic significance. Some researchers propose that humanity's detonation of atomic bombs during the mid-20th century may have attracted extraterrestrial attention, leading to increased UFO activity and incidents like Roswell. This chapter examines the connection between nuclear testing, UFO phenomena, and government secrecy, incorporating high-profile cases such as Gary McKinnon's hacking scandal and Haim Eshed's revelations.

Declassified Documents and Global Perspectives

1. **United States**

- ○ **Project Blue Book (1952–1969)**: This U.S. Air Force program investigated over 12,000 UFO sightings. While most were explained, hundreds remained unidentified, fueling speculation about extraterrestrial involvement and government cover-ups (Ruppelt, 1956).
- ○ **The Pentagon's UAP Report (2021)**: A report by the Office of the Director of National Intelligence analyzed 144 UAP encounters, leaving 143 unexplained. Many incidents involved military installations or nuclear sites, raising concerns about a link between nuclear technology and UFOs (ODNI, 2021).

2. **United Kingdom**

- ○ **The Ministry of Defence (MoD)** declassified thousands of UFO-related files, including reports from nuclear weapons facilities like RAF Bentwaters, where UFOs were allegedly observed tampering with weapon systems (Clarke, 2012).

3. **Soviet Union**

- ○ Soviet records document UFO sightings near nuclear facilities and missile sites. Declassified KGB files describe incidents where UFOs allegedly deactivated nuclear weapons, suggesting a possible extraterrestrial interest in humanity's nuclear arsenal (Popov, 2017).

4.   **Global Patterns**

- ○   Across the globe, UFO activity has frequently been reported near nuclear test sites and weapons facilities, including incidents in Brazil, India, and South Africa (Kean, 2017).

The Roswell Incident and Atomic Testing

1.   **The Historical Context of Nuclear Testing**

- ○   In July 1945, the **Trinity Test**, the first detonation of an atomic bomb, occurred in New Mexico, not far from Roswell. This marked the dawn of the nuclear age and humanity's ability to alter the natural environment on a planetary scale (Rhodes, 1986).
- ○   The theory posits that the energy released by atomic detonations could have propagated into space, signaling to extraterrestrial civilizations that Earth had achieved a destructive technological milestone.

2.   **Roswell as a Response to Nuclear Testing**

- ○   Proponents of the theory argue that the Roswell incident was not coincidental but a direct response to humanity's nuclear activities. The detonation of atomic bombs may have drawn extraterrestrial attention, prompting reconnaissance missions to assess the potential threat posed by humanity (Randle, 1995).

- The timing aligns with increased UFO sightings near nuclear sites, suggesting a pattern of extraterrestrial interest in Earth's nuclear capabilities.

3. **Extraterrestrial Concerns about Nuclear Technology**

- Researchers such as Dr. Steven Greer and L.A. Marzulli have speculated that extraterrestrial civilizations could view nuclear weapons as a danger not only to humanity but to other life forms in the universe. The concept of "nuclear resonance" suggests that atomic detonations could create disturbances beyond Earth, potentially affecting other dimensions or civilizations (Greer, 2017; Marzulli, 2013).

High-Profile Cases of Government Secrecy

1. **Gary McKinnon: NASA Hack and Non-Terrestrial Officers**

- In 2002, UK hacker Gary McKinnon accessed NASA and U.S. military systems, claiming to uncover evidence of "non-terrestrial officers" and spacecraft in orbit (McKinnon, 2004). He also alleged that the government was concealing advanced technologies potentially derived from extraterrestrial sources.
- McKinnon's claims gained credibility due to the difficulty of his feat, though no direct evidence was ever made public.

2.   **Haim Eshed: Galactic Federation**

- In 2020, Haim Eshed, former head of Israel's Defense Ministry's space directorate, claimed that a "Galactic Federation" was monitoring Earth. Eshed suggested that humanity's nuclear advancements were of particular interest to extraterrestrial civilizations, as these technologies pose a potential threat to universal harmony (Eshed, 2020).

Government Cover-Ups and Alleged Evidence

1.   **Project Mogul and the Official Roswell Explanation**

- The U.S. government's official explanation for Roswell centers on **Project Mogul**, a classified program using high-altitude balloons to detect Soviet nuclear tests. While this explanation accounts for some aspects of the incident, many researchers argue it fails to address eyewitness testimony and the alleged recovery of exotic materials (USAF, 1994).

2.   **Alleged Alien Bodies**

- Testimonies from witnesses like Glenn Dennis describe the recovery of non-human remains from the Roswell crash site. These claims, though controversial, align with accounts of extraterrestrial interest in humanity's nuclear capabilities (Dennis & Carey, 1991).

3. Nuclear Site Interventions

- Military personnel have reported UFOs interfering with nuclear weapons systems, including incidents where missiles were rendered inoperative. These events suggest a deliberate effort to monitor or mitigate humanity's use of nuclear technology (Hastings, 2010).

Implications of Extraterrestrial Interest in Nuclear Technology

1. A Warning?

- Some researchers interpret UFO activity near nuclear sites as a warning from extraterrestrial civilizations to prevent humanity from self-destruction. The apparent disabling of nuclear weapons during UFO incidents may indicate an effort to promote peace and stability (Greer, 2017).

2. A Broader Cosmic Perspective

- If extraterrestrial civilizations are aware of humanity's nuclear advancements, it raises questions about our role in the universe. Are we seen as a threat, a curiosity, or a species in need of guidance?

3.   **The Need for Transparency**

- Governments' reluctance to disclose information about UFOs and nuclear incidents has fueled public mistrust. Open disclosure could foster a better understanding of extraterrestrial motives and humanity's place in the cosmos.

Looking Ahead

The intersection of nuclear technology and UFO phenomena continues to intrigue researchers and the public. As more documents are declassified and whistleblowers come forward, the possibility that extraterrestrial civilizations are monitoring humanity's use of atomic weapons offers a compelling lens through which to view events like Roswell.

Sources

1.   Clarke, D. (2012). *The UFO Files: The Inside Story of Real-Life Sightings*. Bloomsbury.
2.   Dennis, G., & Carey, S. (1991). *Witness to Roswell: Unmasking the 60-Year Cover-Up*. New Page Books.
3.   Eshed, H. (2020). Interview with *Yedioth Aharonoth*.
4.   Greer, S. (2017). *Unacknowledged: An Exposé of the World's Greatest Secret*. A&M Publishing.
5.   Hastings, R. (2010). *UFOs and Nukes: Extraordinary Encounters at Nuclear Weapons Sites*. AuthorHouse.

6.   Kean, L. (2017). *UFOs: Generals, Pilots, and Government Officials Go on the Record*. Crown Publishing Group.

7.   McKinnon, G. (2004). Interviews with *BBC Panorama*.

8.   Randle, K. D. (1995). *The Roswell UFO Crash: What They Don't Want You to Know*. Avon Books.

9.   Rhodes, R. (1986). *The Making of the Atomic Bomb*. Simon & Schuster.

10.   USAF. (1994). *The Roswell Report: Fact vs. Fiction in the New Mexico Desert*. U.S. Air Force.

12

The Tic Tac UFO and Modern UAPs

> **The Tic Tac UFO was not behaving by the laws of physics that we know. This was something that was not from this world.** — Commander David Fravor

The "Tic Tac" UFO incident of 2004 is among the most credible and well-documented encounters in modern UFO history. Captured on military radar and witnessed by trained pilots, this unidentified aerial phenomenon (UAP) defied known laws of physics. Alongside this and other recent UAP encounters, evidence suggests that Earth's governments and militaries may possess advanced anti-gravity craft purportedly reverse-engineered from extraterrestrial technology. The U.S. Navy's patented Hybrid Aerospace-Underwater Craft (HAUC) adds further intrigue to this evolving narrative.

The 2004 Tic Tac UFO Incident

1. **Overview**

   ○ The incident occurred off the coast of California, where the USS *Nimitz* Carrier Strike Group detected multiple anomalous objects on radar over several days. These objects exhibited flight characteristics far beyond human technology, such as rapid acceleration, high-speed maneuvers, and hovering without visible propulsion.

- On November 14, 2004, Navy pilots Commander David Fravor and Lieutenant Commander Alex Dietrich were dispatched to intercept one of these objects. They reported seeing a white, oblong object—resembling a "Tic Tac"—that performed maneuvers no known aircraft could achieve (Fravor, 2020).

2.   **Key Features of the Tic Tac UFO**

- **Speed and Acceleration**: The object moved at hypersonic speeds and could accelerate instantaneously.
- **No Visible Means of Propulsion**: It lacked wings, rotors, or exhaust plumes typically associated with aircraft.
- **Underwater and Air Capabilities**: The object was observed descending into the ocean, suggesting advanced underwater capabilities.

3.   **Declassified Footage**

- The encounter was captured on an infrared camera, and the video, along with others (known as the "FLIR1," "Gimbal," and "GoFast" videos), was declassified by the Pentagon in 2020, lending credibility to the pilots' accounts (U.S. Department of Defense, 2020).

Modern UAP Reports

1. **Government Acknowledgment**

      ◦   In June 2021, the Office of the Director of National Intelligence (ODNI) released a report analyzing 144 UAP encounters between 2004 and 2021. Most incidents remained unexplained, with UAPs exhibiting advanced technology that posed potential national security concerns (ODNI, 2021).

2. **Military Whistleblowers**

      ◦   Luis Elizondo, former director of the Pentagon's Advanced Aerospace Threat Identification Program (AATIP), has publicly stated that UAPs demonstrate capabilities far exceeding current human technology, including anti-gravity propulsion and cloaking abilities (Elizondo, 2020).

3. **Global Encounters**

      ◦   Similar UAP incidents have been reported worldwide, including encounters by military pilots in the UK, Russia, and China. These sightings often involve high-speed, high-altitude objects capable of maneuvering in ways that defy known physics.

The Hybrid Aerospace-Underwater Craft (HAUC)

1. **Navy Patent**

   ◦ In 2016, the U.S. Navy filed a patent for the **Hybrid Aerospace-Underwater Craft** (HAUC), which describes a vehicle capable of operating in air, water, and space. The craft purportedly uses an "inertial mass reduction device" to achieve propulsion, which some experts believe is based on anti-gravity principles (Pais, 2016).

2. **Implications of the HAUC Patent**

   ◦ The HAUC patent suggests that advanced propulsion technologies, once considered speculative, may already exist in developmental or operational stages.
   ◦ Critics argue that the patent could be a red herring designed to mislead adversaries or obscure classified programs. However, its filing by a reputable military organization raises questions about the true state of technological advancement.

Reverse-Engineering Extraterrestrial Technology

1. **Historical Claims**

   ◦ Allegations of reverse-engineering extraterrestrial technology date back to the Roswell incident. Whistleblowers such as Bob Lazar have claimed that the U.S. government recovered alien craft and attempted to replicate their propulsion systems (Lazar, 2018).

2.   **Corroborating Testimony**

- ○   Dr. Steven Greer and other researchers have documented accounts from military and intelligence personnel who claim to have worked on reverse-engineering projects. They describe technologies capable of generating anti-gravity effects and extracting energy from the quantum vacuum (Greer, 2017).

3.   **Global Competition**

- ○   Reports suggest that other nations, including Russia and China, are also pursuing advanced propulsion technologies. UAP sightings near military installations could reflect reconnaissance efforts by foreign adversaries or extraterrestrial observers.

The Implications of Anti-Gravity Technology

1.   **Revolutionizing Transportation**

- ○   Anti-gravity propulsion could revolutionize aviation, space exploration, and energy systems. Vehicles powered by such technology would eliminate the need for fossil fuels, dramatically reducing carbon emissions.

2. **Military Dominance**

   - Possession of anti-gravity craft would confer unparalleled military advantages, raising concerns about an arms race involving advanced technologies.

3. **Potential Risks**

   - The secrecy surrounding these technologies could lead to misuse or unintended consequences, particularly if they are weaponized. Transparency and international oversight may be necessary to mitigate these risks.

Skepticism and Alternative Explanations

1. **Natural Phenomena**

   - Some researchers argue that UAPs could be misidentified natural phenomena, such as atmospheric plasma or rare meteorological events.

2. **Human Experimentation**

◦ Others suggest that UAP sightings could reflect classified military programs involving advanced drones or experimental aircraft.

3. **Limitations of Evidence**

◦ While videos and eyewitness accounts are compelling, the lack of physical evidence limits definitive conclusions about the nature of UAPs.

Looking Ahead

The Tic Tac UFO and other UAP encounters represent a turning point in the study of unidentified aerial phenomena. As governments and researchers continue to investigate these incidents, the possibility of reverse-engineered extraterrestrial technology raises profound questions about humanity's technological capabilities and its place in the universe. Whether these craft originate from Earth or beyond, their implications for science, security, and society are nothing short of transformative.

Sources

1. Elizondo, L. (2020). Interviews on *Unidentified: Inside America's UFO Investigation*. History Channel.

2. Fravor, D. (2020). Testimony in *The Phenomenon* documentary. James Fox, Director.

3. Greer, S. (2017). *Unacknowledged: An Exposé of the World's Greatest Secret*. A&M Publishing.

4. Lazar, B. (2018). *Dreamland: An Autobiography*. Interstellar Publishing.

5.   ODNI. (2021). "Preliminary Assessment: Unidentified Aerial Phenomena." Office of the Director of National Intelligence.

6.   Pais, S. T. (2016). U.S. Patent 10144532B2: *Craft Using an Inertial Mass Reduction Device*. U.S. Patent and Trademark Office.

7.   U.S. Department of Defense. (2020). "Declassified UAP Videos." Retrieved from defense.gov.

13

SETI and the Search for Signals

The universe is a pretty big place. If it's just us, seems like an awful waste of space. — Carl Sagan

For decades, scientists have turned their attention to the vast expanse of space, searching for evidence of intelligent extraterrestrial life through signals that could indicate communication. The **Search for Extraterrestrial Intelligence (SETI)** encompasses a variety of efforts to detect electromagnetic signals, such as radio waves or light pulses, from advanced civilizations. This chapter explores the history, methodologies, successes, and challenges of SETI, as well as its implications for humanity's understanding of our place in the universe.

The Origins of SETI

1. **Early Concepts**

   - In 1959, physicists Giuseppe Cocconi and Philip Morrison published a seminal paper in *Nature*, suggesting that extraterrestrial civilizations might use radio waves for interstellar communication. They proposed the 21-centimeter hydrogen line as an ideal frequency for such signals due to its prominence in the universe (Cocconi & Morrison, 1959).

2. **Project Ozma**

- In 1960, Frank Drake conducted the first SETI experiment, **Project Ozma**, at the Green Bank Observatory in West Virginia. Using a 26-meter radio telescope, Drake scanned nearby stars Tau Ceti and Epsilon Eridani for signals. While no signals were detected, the project marked the beginning of systematic SETI research (Drake, 1961).

Key SETI Initiatives

1. **The Arecibo Message (1974)**

- Frank Drake and Carl Sagan designed a binary-coded radio message, transmitted from the Arecibo Observatory in Puerto Rico. The message contained basic information about humanity, including our DNA structure and solar system, directed at the globular star cluster M13. While the message was largely symbolic, it demonstrated the potential for interstellar communication (Sagan, 1974).

2. **Breakthrough Listen (2015–Present)**

- Funded by billionaire Yuri Milner, Breakthrough Listen is the most comprehensive SETI program to date, scanning millions of stars across multiple frequencies. Using facilities like the Green Bank Telescope and Parkes Observatory, the project represents a new era in SETI research with unprecedented data-gathering capabilities (Worden et al., 2016).

3. **Laser SETI**

- Traditional SETI searches focus on radio signals, but **Laser SETI** explores the possibility that extraterrestrial civilizations might use optical or infrared light pulses for communication. These signals could travel vast distances with minimal interference, offering another avenue for detection (Howard et al., 2004).

4. **The Allen Telescope Array (ATA)**

- Located in California, the ATA is a network of 42 radio telescopes dedicated to SETI research. Unlike single-dish observatories, the ATA can simultaneously scan multiple regions of the sky, increasing the likelihood of detecting signals (Tarter, 2001).

Methodologies in SETI

1. **Targeted Searches**

- Targeted searches focus on specific stars or regions, often selecting those with known exoplanets in the habitable zone. The Kepler and TESS missions have identified thousands of such planets, providing promising targets for SETI (NASA, 2023).

2.   **All-Sky Surveys**

○   These surveys scan broad areas of the sky, searching for signals from any direction. While less precise, all-sky surveys maximize coverage and are particularly useful for detecting transient signals.

3.   **Artificial Intelligence (AI)**

○   AI algorithms are increasingly used to analyze SETI data, identifying patterns or anomalies that might be missed by traditional methods. AI was instrumental in re-analyzing data from Breakthrough Listen, uncovering previously unnoticed signals (Zhang et al., 2021).

Notable Signals

1.   **The Wow! Signal (1977)**

○   Detected by Jerry Ehman at Ohio State University's Big Ear Radio Telescope, the **Wow! Signal** was a strong, narrowband radio signal that appeared artificial in origin.

Despite extensive follow-up efforts, the signal was never detected again, leaving its origin a mystery (Gray, 2011).

2. **FRB 121102**

- This repeating fast radio burst (FRB) was discovered in 2016. While FRBs are likely natural phenomena, their precise nature remains unclear, and some researchers speculate that advanced civilizations might produce them intentionally (Spitler et al., 2016).

Challenges in SETI

1. **Signal Detection and Noise**

- The vastness of space and the weakness of potential signals make detection challenging. Earth-based radio interference, known as "terrestrial noise," complicates efforts to distinguish alien signals from human-made ones.

2. **Fermi's Paradox**

- Despite decades of searching, SETI has yet to produce conclusive evidence of extraterrestrial communication. This lack of success amplifies Fermi's Paradox: *If extraterrestrial civilizations exist, why haven't we detected them?* (Hart, 1975).

3.   **Limited Funding**

○   SETI research has historically struggled with funding. Programs like Breakthrough Listen rely on private investments, as public funding for SETI remains scarce.

Implications of SETI

1.   **Scientific Breakthroughs**

○   Detecting an alien signal would revolutionize our understanding of science, particularly in fields like physics, biology, and engineering. Decoding the signal could reveal insights into advanced technologies and universal principles.

2.   **Philosophical and Cultural Impact**

○   The discovery of extraterrestrial intelligence would challenge humanity's view of itself, reshaping religion, philosophy, and culture. As Carl Sagan observed, *"For small creatures such as we, the vastness is bearable only through love."* (Sagan, 1994).

3.   **Global Cooperation**

◦ A confirmed detection would necessitate international collaboration to interpret the signal and establish protocols for potential communication. SETI could serve as a unifying force, fostering a sense of shared purpose across nations.

Looking Ahead

SETI is poised to enter a new era of discovery, driven by advances in technology and growing interest in the search for extraterrestrial life. As telescopes like the James Webb Space Telescope and the Square Kilometre Array come online, the likelihood of detecting a signal increases. Whether we find ourselves alone or part of a cosmic community, SETI ensures that humanity will continue to explore the great unknown.

Sources

1. Cocconi, G., & Morrison, P. (1959). "Searching for Interstellar Communications." *Nature*, 184(4690), 844–846.
2. Drake, F. (1961). "Project Ozma." *Physics Today*, 14(4).
3. Gray, R. (2011). *The Elusive Wow: Searching for Extraterrestrial Intelligence*. Palmer Square Press.
4. Howard, A., et al. (2004). "Laser SETI: A Search for Artificially Generated Optical Pulses." *The Astrophysical Journal*, 613(2), 1270–1284.
5. NASA. (2023). "Exoplanet Exploration." Retrieved from exoplanets.nasa.gov.
6. Sagan, C. (1994). *Pale Blue Dot: A Vision of the Human Future in Space*. Random House.
7. Spitler, L. G., et al. (2016). "A Repeating Fast Radio Burst." *Nature*, 531(7593), 202–205.

8.   Tarter, J. (2001). "The Search for Extraterrestrial Intelligence (SETI)." *Annual Review of Astronomy and Astrophysics*, 39, 511–548.

9.   Worden, P., et al. (2016). "Breakthrough Listen: A New Search for ET." *Publications of the Astronomical Society of the Pacific*, 128(959).

10.   Zhang, Z., et al. (2021). "AI-Driven Search for Technosignatures in Breakthrough Listen Data." *Nature Astronomy*, 5, 123–129.

Part III: Imagining Contact

14

First Contact Scenarios

First contact with extraterrestrials will be the most transformative moment in human history, altering everything from science to spirituality. — Dr. Steven Greer

The question of how humanity might encounter extraterrestrial life has long fascinated scientists, philosophers, and researchers. From peaceful communication to catastrophic invasion, a variety of first contact scenarios have been proposed. This chapter explores how scientists and researchers, including Dr. Tom Horn, Cris Putnam, Dr. Steven Greer, L.A. Marzulli, Gary Stearman, and Dr. Michael Salla, envision humanity's potential encounters with alien civilizations.

Types of First Contact Scenarios

1. **Remote Detection**

   - Humanity might first detect extraterrestrials through signals or technosignatures, such as radio waves or laser pulses. This form of contact would be indirect, involving long-distance communication rather than physical interaction (Cocconi & Morrison, 1959).
   - The work of SETI (Search for Extraterrestrial Intelligence) highlights this possibility, with programs like Break-

through Listen scanning the skies for evidence of intelligent life (Worden et al., 2016).

2. **Physical Visitation**

- Alien spacecraft arriving on Earth is a common scenario in both scientific speculation and popular culture. Researchers like Dr. Steven Greer suggest that such visitations may already be occurring, citing documented UFO sightings and whistleblower testimony (Greer, 2017).
- L.A. Marzulli, in his *Watchers* series, argues that some UFO sightings and abduction cases could involve physical encounters with non-human entities, possibly with a spiritual dimension (Marzulli, 2013).

3. **Discovery in Our Solar System**

- Humanity might encounter microbial or even complex life on nearby planets or moons, such as Mars, Europa, or Enceladus. This scenario would involve scientific exploration rather than interstellar contact, but its implications would still be profound (NASA, 2023).

4. **Post-Detection Communication**

- In this scenario, humanity receives a deliberate signal from an alien civilization, initiating a communication process. The challenges would include decoding the message and determining the intent behind it (Vakoch, 2014).

Perspectives on First Contact

1. **Dr. Steven Greer**

   - Greer emphasizes the need for peaceful and proactive contact. He argues that extraterrestrials are likely observing humanity and waiting for us to demonstrate a commitment to peace and sustainability.
   - In *Close Encounters of the Fifth Kind* (2020), Greer outlines methods for initiating contact through meditation and consciousness-based practices, asserting that advanced civilizations might communicate telepathically or through higher-dimensional means.

2. **Dr. Tom Horn and Cris Putnam**

   - In *Exo-Vaticana* (2013), Horn and Putnam discussed the theological implications of extraterrestrial contact, suggesting that the Vatican may anticipate such an event. They speculated that extraterrestrials could be perceived as "saviors" or "messengers" by humanity, potentially reshaping religious beliefs.
   - Horn and Putnam also warned of deception, proposing that some entities might present themselves as benevolent while pursuing hidden agendas.

3.   **L.A. Marzulli**

- ◦   Marzulli explores the possibility that first contact might involve entities with malevolent intent, linking modern UFO phenomena to the Nephilim described in biblical texts (Marzulli, 2013). He theorizes that these entities may attempt to deceive humanity by masquerading as extraterrestrials while carrying out spiritual or demonic agendas.

4.   **Gary Stearman**

- ◦   Stearman, a biblical scholar, views potential first contact as a fulfillment of prophetic events. He suggests that extraterrestrial encounters could coincide with apocalyptic scenarios, drawing parallels between UFO activity and biblical accounts of angelic beings (Stearman, 2012).

5.   **Dr. Michael Salla**

- ◦   Salla, a proponent of exopolitics, envisions first contact as a diplomatic challenge. In *Exopolitics: Political Implications of the Extraterrestrial Presence* (2004), he argues that humanity must prepare for interstellar diplomacy, including developing frameworks for negotiation and cooperation with extraterrestrial civilizations.

Challenges and Risks of First Contact

1. **Communication Barriers**

   ° Extraterrestrials may have entirely different modes of communication, such as visual signals, mathematical patterns, or telepathy. Decoding their messages could be an enormous challenge (Vakoch, 2014).

2. **Technological Disparity**

   ° Contact with a more advanced civilization could pose risks, including the potential for exploitation or cultural domination. Stephen Hawking famously warned that meeting extraterrestrials might mirror historical encounters between colonizers and indigenous peoples, often with catastrophic results (Hawking, 2010).

3. **Psychological and Societal Impact**

   ° First contact could provoke widespread fear or disrupt societal structures, particularly if extraterrestrials challenge existing religious or philosophical beliefs. Marzulli and Horn highlight the potential for spiritual deception in such scenarios.

4. **Hostile Intent**

- The possibility of hostile extraterrestrials cannot be ruled out. Advanced civilizations might view humanity as a threat or a resource, leading to scenarios of invasion or subjugation.

Protocols for First Contact

1. **The Rio Scale**

    - Developed by SETI researchers, the Rio Scale evaluates the significance and credibility of a potential extraterrestrial signal, guiding public and scientific responses (Almar & Tarter, 2000).

2. **United Nations Guidelines**

    - While no formal global protocols exist, the United Nations has discussed the need for international cooperation in the event of first contact. The Outer Space Treaty of 1967 provides a legal framework for space exploration, emphasizing peaceful purposes (UNOOSA, 1967).

3. **Cultural and Religious Preparation**

    - Horn and Putnam suggested that religious institutions, particularly the Vatican, may play a crucial role in interpreting the implications of first contact for humanity's spiritual understanding.

Implications of First Contact

1.   Scientific Advancements

- ○   Interacting with an advanced civilization could lead to breakthroughs in physics, biology, and energy systems. Dr. Greer argues that extraterrestrial technology might provide solutions to humanity's greatest challenges, including climate change and energy scarcity (Greer, 2017).

2.   Global Unity

- ○   First contact could unify humanity by providing a shared purpose and a broader perspective on our place in the universe. As Carl Sagan noted, *"For small creatures such as we, the vastness is bearable only through love."*

3.   Philosophical and Spiritual Evolution

- ○   Encountering extraterrestrials would challenge humanity to redefine concepts of life, intelligence, and morality. Researchers like Marzulli and Stearman emphasize the need to approach such encounters with discernment, given the potential for deception.

Looking Ahead

As scientific efforts like SETI continue and public interest in UFO phenomena grows, the prospect of first contact becomes increasingly plausible. Whether it occurs through a distant signal, physical visitation, or a sudden revelation, humanity must prepare for the transformative implications of meeting our cosmic neighbors.

Sources

1. Cocconi, G., & Morrison, P. (1959). "Searching for Interstellar Communications." *Nature*, 184(4690), 844–846.

2. Greer, S. (2017). *Unacknowledged: An Exposé of the World's Greatest Secret*. A&M Publishing.

3. Hawking, S. (2010). Interview on *Into the Universe with Stephen Hawking*. Discovery Channel.

4. Horn, T., & Putnam, C. (2013). *Exo-Vaticana: Petrus Romanus, Project Lucifer, and the Vatican's Astonishing Plan for the Arrival of an Alien Savior*. Defender Publishing.

5. Marzulli, L. A. (2013). *The Watchers Series* [Film Series]. Spiral of Life.

6. NASA. (2023). "Exoplanet Exploration." Retrieved from exoplanets.nasa.gov.

7. Salla, M. (2004). *Exopolitics: Political Implications of the Extraterrestrial Presence*. Exopolitics Institute.

8. Stearman, G. (2012). *Prophecy Watchers: Aliens and Angels*. Prophecy Watchers Media.

9. Vakoch, D. A. (2014). *Extraterrestrial Altruism: Evolution and Ethics in the Cosmos*. Springer.

10. Worden, P., et al. (2016). "Breakthrough Listen: A New Search for ET." *Publications of the Astronomical Society of the Pacific*, 128(959).

15

The Cultural Impact of ETs

> Science fiction is the mythology of modernity, and extraterrestrials are its gods.
> — Carl Sagan

Aliens have fascinated humanity for centuries, but it is through books, movies, and art that their presence has deeply imprinted on our collective imagination. These cultural mediums have not only shaped how we perceive extraterrestrials but have also reflected our hopes, fears, and evolving understanding of science and the cosmos. This chapter explores the cultural impact of aliens in literature, cinema, and art, examining how these portrayals have influenced society's expectations about extraterrestrial life.

The Evolution of Aliens in Literature

1. **Early Literary Representations**

   - In 1898, H.G. Wells' *The War of the Worlds* introduced the concept of alien invasion, reflecting fears of colonization and technological supremacy. Wells' Martians were both terrifying and advanced, representing humanity's anxieties about the industrial age (Wells, 1898).
   - Jules Verne's *From the Earth to the Moon* (1865) and Edgar Rice Burroughs' *A Princess of Mars* (1912) depicted

space exploration and extraterrestrial encounters as adventures, laying the groundwork for optimistic portrayals of aliens.

2. **Post-War Reflections**

- The Cold War era saw a surge in science fiction, with books like Arthur C. Clarke's *Childhood's End* (1953) and Ray Bradbury's *The Martian Chronicles* (1950) exploring themes of nuclear war, colonization, and the evolution of humanity in the context of alien contact.
- Isaac Asimov's *Foundation* series (1951) envisioned a galaxy teeming with advanced civilizations, highlighting humanity's role in a broader cosmic ecosystem.

3. **Modern Portrayals**

- Contemporary works like Ted Chiang's *Story of Your Life* (1998), adapted into the film *Arrival*, explore the complexities of alien communication and the philosophical implications of contact (Chiang, 1998).
- In fiction like Liu Cixin's *The Three-Body Problem* (2008), aliens are portrayed as morally ambiguous, challenging humanity's assumptions about cooperation and conflict.

Aliens in Cinema

1. **The Early Years**

   ○ The 1950s saw the rise of alien-themed B-movies, often reflecting Cold War paranoia. Films like *The Day the Earth Stood Still* (1951) presented extraterrestrials as warnings to humanity about the dangers of war and environmental destruction (Wise, 1951).

   ○ *Invasion of the Body Snatchers* (1956) explored themes of conformity and the loss of individuality, mirroring fears of Communist infiltration during the McCarthy era.

2. **Blockbusters and Pop Culture Icons**

   ○ Steven Spielberg's *Close Encounters of the Third Kind* (1977) and *E.T. the Extra-Terrestrial* (1982) portrayed aliens as benevolent beings, emphasizing communication and empathy over conflict.

   ○ In contrast, films like *Independence Day* (1996) and *Alien* (1979) depicted extraterrestrials as hostile invaders or predatory life forms, playing on humanity's fears of the unknown.

3. **Modern Narratives**

   ○ Recent films like *Arrival* (2016) focus on the challenges of understanding alien languages and perspectives, emphasizing intellectual and emotional growth over violence.

○ *Avatar* (2009) explores themes of colonization and environmental stewardship, presenting humans as the invaders and aliens as the custodians of a fragile ecosystem.

Aliens in Art

1. Visual Art and Symbolism

○ From Renaissance paintings depicting celestial objects to surrealist interpretations of alien landscapes, artists have long imagined extraterrestrial realms. Works like Salvador Dalí's *The Persistence of Memory* (1931) evoke otherworldly dimensions, indirectly reflecting themes of alien otherness.

2. Contemporary Alien Art

○ Artists like H.R. Giger, whose biomechanical designs shaped the *Alien* franchise, created haunting visions of extraterrestrial life that blended organic and technological elements. Giger's work highlights humanity's fascination—and fear—of the unfamiliar (Giger, 1979).

3. Street Art and Pop Culture

○ Alien imagery has permeated urban art, with street murals and graffiti often featuring depictions of UFOs, aliens, and space travel. These works reflect society's enduring interest in the mystery of extraterrestrial life.

Themes and Motifs in Alien Media

1. **Aliens as Mirrors of Humanity**

    ◦   Many portrayals of extraterrestrials serve as reflections of human traits, values, and flaws. Benevolent aliens like those in *E.T.* highlight empathy and connection, while malevolent ones like the Xenomorph in *Alien* symbolize primal fears of survival and reproduction.

2. **Technology and Progress**

    ◦   Alien narratives often explore humanity's relationship with technology. Advanced civilizations in films like *Contact* (1997) challenge humanity to evolve intellectually and spiritually, while others warn of the dangers of technological hubris.

3. **Exploration and the Unknown**

    ◦   Aliens are frequently used to represent the broader human quest for knowledge and exploration. Stories like *Star Trek* emphasize cooperation and curiosity, framing extraterrestrial encounters as opportunities for mutual growth.

Commentary by Key Figures

1.   **Dr. Steven Greer**

      ◦   Greer views media portrayals of aliens as overly influenced by fear and sensationalism. He argues that most extraterrestrial civilizations are likely peaceful and that humanity's media-driven fear of aliens hinders meaningful contact (Greer, 2017).

2.   **Dr. Tom Horn and Cris Putnam**

      ◦   In *Exo-Vaticana* (2013), Horn and Putnam, both deceased, discussed how media portrayals of extraterrestrials could prime humanity for potential deception. They warned that narratives depicting aliens as saviors could be used to manipulate public opinion during a real or staged contact event.

3.   **L.A. Marzulli**

      ◦   Marzulli argues that alien-themed media often glamorizes extraterrestrial encounters while ignoring their potentially malevolent nature. He suggests that such portrayals align with spiritual deception and biblical prophecy (Marzulli, 2013).

4. **Dr. Michael Salla**

   ° Salla emphasizes the importance of positive narratives, suggesting that media can prepare humanity for peaceful contact by promoting themes of diplomacy and cooperation (Salla, 2004).

Implications of Alien Media on Society

1. **Shaping Public Perception**

   ° Films and books about aliens influence public expectations, shaping how humanity might react to real-life extraterrestrial contact.
   ° A study by Vakoch (2014) highlights how science fiction can prepare individuals to think critically about complex issues like communication and ethics.

2. **Driving Scientific Curiosity**

   ° Cultural depictions of aliens often inspire interest in astronomy, space exploration, and astrobiology, fostering scientific innovation and exploration.

3. **Philosophical and Spiritual Reflection**

   ◦ Alien narratives challenge humanity to consider its place in the universe and its moral responsibilities as a potentially cosmic species.

Looking Ahead

As humanity moves closer to discovering extraterrestrial life, whether through scientific exploration or contact, the cultural narratives surrounding aliens will continue to shape our collective response. The stories we tell today may influence how we engage with the realities of tomorrow.

Sources

1. Chiang, T. (1998). *Story of Your Life*. Tor Books.
2. Cocconi, G., & Morrison, P. (1959). "Searching for Interstellar Communications." *Nature*, 184(4690), 844–846.
3. Greer, S. (2017). *Unacknowledged: An Exposé of the World's Greatest Secret*. A&M Publishing.
4. Giger, H. R. (1979). *Alien Designs*. Twentieth Century Fox.
5. Horn, T., & Putnam, C. (2013). *Exo-Vaticana: Petrus Romanus, Project Lucifer, and the Vatican's Astonishing Plan for the Arrival of an Alien Savior*. Defender Publishing.
6. Marzulli, L. A. (2013). *The Watchers Series*. Spiral of Life.
7. Salla, M. (2004). *Exopolitics: Political Implications of the Extraterrestrial Presence*. Exopolitics Institute.
8. Vakoch, D. A. (2014). *Extraterrestrial Altruism: Evolution and Ethics in the Cosmos*. Springer.

9.   Wells, H. G. (1898). *The War of the Worlds*. William Heinemann.

10.   Wise, R. (Director). (1951). *The Day the Earth Stood Still*. Twentieth Century Fox.

16

Friend or Foe?

> The motives of extraterrestrial visitors may range from benevolence to indifference to outright hostility. Understanding their intentions is one of humanity's greatest challenges.
> — Dr. Michael Salla

If humanity were to encounter extraterrestrial civilizations, one of the most pressing questions would be their intentions. Are they peaceful explorers seeking knowledge and connection, or are they a potential threat to humanity's survival? This chapter explores the spectrum of possible motives for extraterrestrial visitors, incorporating scientific, philosophical, and theological perspectives as well as insights from researchers like Dr. Michael Salla, Dr. Steven Greer, Dr. Tom Horn, and L.A. Marzulli.

The Benevolent Visitor

1. **Explorers and Diplomats**

   - Extraterrestrial civilizations may visit Earth out of curiosity or a desire to exchange knowledge and culture.
   - Dr. Steven Greer argues that many advanced civilizations are likely peaceful, having overcome the destructive tendencies that threaten their survival. He suggests that

their primary motive could be to guide humanity toward sustainable development and interstellar cooperation (Greer, 2017).

2.   **Protectors of the Cosmos**

- °   Advanced extraterrestrials might see themselves as guardians of the galaxy, intervening to ensure the stability of planetary ecosystems.
- °   The theory that UFOs have been observed near nuclear facilities supports this idea. Researchers like Robert Hastings document cases where unidentified objects reportedly disabled nuclear weapons, potentially as a warning against their use (Hastings, 2010).

3.   **Catalysts for Human Evolution**

- °   Some theorists propose that extraterrestrials might seek to accelerate humanity's intellectual, spiritual, or technological evolution.
- °   Dr. Michael Salla suggests that contact could lead to the disclosure of advanced technologies, such as zero-point energy, that could address global challenges like climate change and poverty (Salla, 2004).

The Neutral Observer

1. **Scientific Research**

   ○ Just as humans study animal behavior and ecosystems, extraterrestrials may be studying Earth as part of a broader scientific mission.
   ○ This perspective aligns with the **Zoo Hypothesis**, which suggests that Earth is a controlled environment where extraterrestrials observe without interfering (Ball, 1973).

2. **Indifference to Humanity**

   ○ Advanced civilizations might view humanity as inconsequential or primitive, focusing instead on larger cosmic phenomena.
   ○ Carl Sagan argued that extraterrestrials capable of interstellar travel would likely be more interested in understanding the universe than in engaging with a single species on a small planet (Sagan, 1994).

The Malevolent Visitor

1. **Resource Exploitation**

   ○ A darker possibility is that extraterrestrials might seek Earth's resources, including water, minerals, or even biological material.

○ In *The Three-Body Problem* (2008), Liu Cixin explores the idea of an alien civilization viewing humanity as expendable in their quest for survival, reflecting humanity's own history of colonization.

2.   Hostility Toward Humanity

○ L.A. Marzulli argues that extraterrestrial encounters might involve malevolent entities masquerading as advanced beings. Drawing on biblical references to the Nephilim, Marzulli suggests that some alien visitors could have deceptive or destructive motives (Marzulli, 2013).

○ Historical narratives, such as H.G. Wells' *The War of the Worlds* (1898), reflect fears of technologically superior civilizations exploiting or annihilating humanity.

3.   Existential Threats

○ Stephen Hawking warned that contact with extraterrestrials could lead to outcomes similar to historical encounters between colonizers and indigenous peoples, often resulting in the latter's destruction. He suggested that alien civilizations might view humanity as a threat or an opportunity for domination (Hawking, 2010).

Mixed Motives and Complexity

1. **Diverse Civilizations**

   - Just as humanity consists of diverse cultures with varying motives, extraterrestrial civilizations may not have a unified agenda. Different factions or species could have conflicting goals regarding Earth.
   - Dr. Tom Horn and Cris Putnam proposed that some extraterrestrial entities might present themselves as saviors, offering advanced technology or spiritual guidance, while others might have hidden, self-serving motives (Horn & Putnam, 2013).

2. **Unintended Consequences**

   - Even well-meaning extraterrestrial actions could have negative impacts on humanity, such as cultural disruption, technological dependency, or ecological harm.

Determining Intentions

1. **Signs of Benevolence**

   - Efforts to communicate, share knowledge, or mitigate global risks could indicate friendly intentions. For example, sightings of UFOs near nuclear sites might reflect an interest in preventing planetary self-destruction.

2. **Signs of Hostility**

- ○ Aggressive actions, such as disabling satellites, attacking infrastructure, or harming individuals, would suggest malevolent motives.
- ○ Researchers like Gary Stearman emphasize the need for discernment, cautioning against assuming that all extraterrestrial encounters are benign (Stearman, 2012).

3. **The Role of Communication**

- ○ Decoding alien messages and understanding their language or intentions would be critical. Dr. Douglas Vakoch highlights the challenges of interpreting signals from civilizations with entirely different cognitive frameworks (Vakoch, 2014).

Implications for Humanity

1. **Ethical and Philosophical Challenges**

- ○ Encountering extraterrestrials would force humanity to confront questions about morality, coexistence, and the nature of intelligence.
- ○ Theological interpretations, such as those by Marzulli and Stearman, suggest that contact could either affirm or challenge religious beliefs.

2. **Global Unity or Division**

- A shared encounter with extraterrestrials could unite humanity under a common purpose or exacerbate divisions based on fear and competition.
- The response to extraterrestrial contact would likely depend on the transparency and cooperation of governments and institutions.

3. **A Test of Human Values**

- Humanity's ability to approach extraterrestrial contact with curiosity, humility, and caution could shape the outcome of such encounters. As Carl Sagan observed, *"In a cosmic perspective, each of us is precious. If a human disagrees with you, let him live. In a hundred billion galaxies, you will not find another."*

Looking Ahead

Understanding the potential motives of extraterrestrial visitors is not only a matter of speculation but a necessary exercise in preparedness. Whether friend, foe, or something in between, extraterrestrial contact would challenge humanity to respond with wisdom and unity, navigating the complexities of an encounter that could redefine our place in the universe.

Sources

1. Ball, J. A. (1973). "The Zoo Hypothesis." *Icarus*, 19(3), 347–349.

2. Greer, S. (2017). *Unacknowledged: An Exposé of the World's Greatest Secret*. A&M Publishing.

3. Hastings, R. (2010). *UFOs and Nukes: Extraordinary Encounters at Nuclear Weapons Sites*. AuthorHouse.

4. Hawking, S. (2010). Interview on *Into the Universe with Stephen Hawking*. Discovery Channel.

5. Horn, T., & Putnam, C. (2013). *Exo-Vaticana: Petrus Romanus, Project Lucifer, and the Vatican's Astonishing Plan for the Arrival of an Alien Savior*. Defender Publishing.

6. Marzulli, L. A. (2013). *The Watchers Series*. Spiral of Life.

7. Sagan, C. (1994). *Pale Blue Dot: A Vision of the Human Future in Space*. Random House.

8. Salla, M. (2004). *Exopolitics: Political Implications of the Extraterrestrial Presence*. Exopolitics Institute.

9. Vakoch, D. A. (2014). *Extraterrestrial Altruism: Evolution and Ethics in the Cosmos*. Springer.

10. Wells, H. G. (1898). *The War of the Worlds*. William Heinemann.

17

Alien Technology

> **Any sufficiently advanced technology is indistinguishable from magic.**
> — Arthur C. Clarke

The discovery of alien technology would revolutionize human understanding of science and engineering. Such technology, potentially far beyond our current capabilities, could solve global challenges, reshape industries, and transform society. This chapter explores the theoretical advances in alien technology, their possible mechanisms, and their profound implications for humanity.

Theoretical Alien Technologies

1. **Faster-Than-Light Travel**

    - **Warp Drives:** Inspired by Einstein's theory of relativity, theoretical warp drives could allow spacecraft to travel faster than light by bending spacetime.

        - Physicist Miguel Alcubierre proposed a model in 1994 for a warp bubble that compresses space ahead of a craft and expands it behind (Alcubierre, 1994).

- Alien civilizations capable of interstellar travel may have mastered this concept, overcoming the immense energy requirements through advanced physics.
  - **Wormholes**: Another theoretical approach involves traversable wormholes, which could serve as shortcuts through spacetime. Researchers like Kip Thorne have explored the plausibility of stable wormholes using exotic matter (Thorne, 1994).

2. **Anti-Gravity Propulsion**

  - Alien spacecraft observed in UFO sightings often display flight characteristics suggestive of anti-gravity propulsion, such as hovering without visible means of support and abrupt changes in direction.
  - The U.S. Navy's patent for the **Hybrid Aerospace-Underwater Craft (HAUC)** describes a craft using "inertial mass reduction" for propulsion, possibly inspired by observations of advanced extraterrestrial technology (Pais, 2016).

3. **Unlimited Energy Sources**

  - **Zero-Point Energy**: Alien civilizations may have harnessed vacuum energy, a theoretical source of limitless energy derived from quantum fluctuations in empty space.

- Dr. Steven Greer argues that extraterrestrial technology could provide clean, renewable energy, eliminating humanity's dependence on fossil fuels (Greer, 2017).
  - **Dyson Spheres**: A Type II civilization on the Kardashev Scale might construct a Dyson Sphere, a megastructure surrounding a star to capture its energy output. This concept, proposed by physicist Freeman Dyson, represents an efficient way to sustain an advanced society (Dyson, 1960).

4. **Advanced Materials**

  - **Meta-Materials**: Alleged UFO crash sites, such as Roswell, have been associated with materials exhibiting extraordinary properties, such as memory metal and materials capable of manipulating light (Marcel, 1980; Kean, 2017).
  - **Self-Healing Alloys**: Alien technology may include self-repairing materials that can regenerate after sustaining damage, ensuring durability and longevity in extreme environments.

5. **Artificial Intelligence and Consciousness Integration**

  - Advanced alien civilizations may have merged biological and artificial intelligence, creating entities capable of extraordinary cognitive abilities.

- Dr. Michael Salla suggests that extraterrestrial AI might be involved in interstellar exploration, operating as autonomous probes or as extensions of advanced beings (Salla, 2004).

Potential Mechanisms Behind Alien Technology

1. Unified Physics

- Alien civilizations may have developed a unified theory of physics, integrating quantum mechanics and general relativity. This understanding could unlock technologies that appear impossible to humanity, such as manipulating spacetime and generating immense amounts of energy.

2. Dimensional Manipulation

- Some researchers propose that extraterrestrials operate across higher dimensions, enabling them to traverse great distances or remain undetectable to human senses.
- L.A. Marzulli suggests that such beings might use interdimensional travel as a means of interacting with or observing Earth (Marzulli, 2013).

3. Bioengineering and Genetic Advancements

○ Alien technology might include advanced bioengineering tools capable of creating or modifying life forms for specific purposes, such as space exploration or environmental adaptation.

Implications for Humanity

1. **Scientific Advancements**

   ○ Reverse-engineering alien technology could lead to breakthroughs in propulsion, energy, materials science, and medicine.
   ○ Such advancements might allow humanity to achieve interstellar travel, colonize other planets, and address global crises like climate change.

2. **Societal Transformation**

   ○ Alien technology could disrupt existing economic and political systems by rendering current industries obsolete. For example, zero-point energy could eliminate the need for oil, coal, and natural gas, reshaping global geopolitics.

3. **Ethical and Security Concerns**

   ○ Access to powerful alien technology could lead to misuse or weaponization. Governments and institutions would face the challenge of ensuring equitable distribution and preventing destructive applications.

4. Cultural and Philosophical Shifts

- Encountering technology far beyond human capabilities would challenge humanity's perception of its place in the universe. It might inspire awe and humility while raising existential questions about the limits of human potential.

Challenges in Understanding Alien Technology

1. Technological Disparity

- Alien technology may be so advanced that it appears incomprehensible or indistinguishable from magic, as Clarke's Third Law suggests.
- Decoding such technology would require a multidisciplinary approach, combining physics, engineering, and computational science.

2. Secrecy and Access

- Allegations of government concealment, such as claims by Bob Lazar about reverse-engineering alien craft at Area

51, highlight the difficulty of obtaining verifiable evidence (Lazar, 2018).

3.   **Ethical Considerations**

- ○   Researchers and policymakers would need to address the ethical implications of using alien technology, particularly if it involves materials or mechanisms that challenge human understanding of life and consciousness.

Insights from Key Figures

1.   **Dr. Steven Greer**

- ○   Greer advocates for the public disclosure of alien technology, arguing that its potential to solve global problems outweighs the risks of secrecy (Greer, 2017).

2.   **Dr. Michael Salla**

- ○   Salla emphasizes the importance of transparency and international collaboration in studying alien technology. He warns against the monopolization of such advancements by a single government or corporation (Salla, 2004).

3.   **L.A. Marzulli**

   ◦   Marzulli cautions against assuming that all alien technology is benevolent. He argues that its origins and motives must be carefully examined to avoid spiritual or societal harm (Marzulli, 2013).

Looking Ahead

The discovery and integration of alien technology would be a turning point in human history, offering both immense opportunities and significant challenges. As researchers and policymakers continue to explore this possibility, humanity must approach the subject with a balance of curiosity, caution, and responsibility, ensuring that such advancements benefit all of civilization.

Sources

1.   Alcubierre, M. (1994). "The Warp Drive: Hyper-Fast Travel Within General Relativity." *Classical and Quantum Gravity*, 11(5), L73–L77.
2.   Dyson, F. (1960). "Search for Artificial Stellar Sources of Infrared Radiation." *Science*, 131(3414), 1667–1668.
3.   Greer, S. (2017). *Unacknowledged: An Exposé of the World's Greatest Secret*. A&M Publishing.
4.   Hastings, R. (2010). *UFOs and Nukes: Extraordinary Encounters at Nuclear Weapons Sites*. AuthorHouse.
5.   Kean, L. (2017). *UFOs: Generals, Pilots, and Government Officials Go on the Record*. Crown Publishing Group.
6.   Lazar, B. (2018). *Dreamland: An Autobiography*. Interstellar Publishing.
7.   Marzulli, L. A. (2013). *The Watchers Series*. Spiral of Life.

8.	Pais, S. T. (2016). U.S. Patent 10144532B2: *Craft Using an Inertial Mass Reduction Device*. U.S. Patent and Trademark Office.

9.	Salla, M. (2004). *Exopolitics: Political Implications of the Extraterrestrial Presence*. Exopolitics Institute.

10.	Thorne, K. S. (1994). *Black Holes and Time Warps: Einstein's Outrageous Legacy*. W.W. Norton & Company.

18

Interstellar Travel

The distances between stars are immense, but for a civilization with advanced technology, they may represent challenges, not barriers.
— Dr. Michio Kaku

One of the greatest mysteries surrounding extraterrestrial civilizations is how they might traverse the vast distances of space. For humans, even the nearest stars are unreachable with current propulsion technology. However, advanced extraterrestrial species could possess interstellar travel capabilities that far exceed our understanding. This chapter explores the theoretical methods ETs might use to overcome these immense distances, including warp drives, wormholes, and other speculative technologies.

The Challenges of Interstellar Travel

1. **Immense Distances**

   - The closest star system, **Alpha Centauri**, is 4.37 light-years away, equating to approximately 25 trillion miles. Even with our fastest spacecraft, it would take tens of thousands of years to reach.

2.   **Energy Requirements**

- ◦   Conventional propulsion systems require enormous amounts of energy to achieve significant fractions of the speed of light. The theoretical energy demands for interstellar travel are beyond current human capabilities (NASA, 2023).

3.   **Relativistic Effects**

- ◦   Traveling near the speed of light introduces time dilation, where time passes more slowly for the traveler than for those at their origin. While this could benefit long-distance journeys, it complicates communication and synchronization with the home planet (Einstein, 1905).

Theoretical Methods of Interstellar Travel

1.   **Warp Drives**

- ◦   Proposed by Miguel Alcubierre in 1994, a warp drive theoretically allows a spacecraft to contract space in front of it and expand space behind it, creating a "warp bubble."
- ◦   The spacecraft itself does not move through space but is carried along the distorted spacetime. This could enable faster-than-light travel without violating Einstein's theory of relativity (Alcubierre, 1994).
- ◦   Challenges include the need for exotic matter with negative energy density to stabilize the warp bubble. Some re-

cent studies suggest that small-scale warp drives might be feasible with further advancements in quantum field theory (Lentz, 2021).

2.   **Wormholes**

- ◦   Wormholes, or Einstein-Rosen bridges, are theoretical shortcuts through spacetime that could connect distant regions of the universe.
- ◦   While theoretically possible, maintaining a stable, traversable wormhole requires exotic matter to prevent collapse. Physicist Kip Thorne has explored these possibilities, linking them to general relativity and quantum mechanics (Thorne, 1994).

3.   **Light Sails and Laser Propulsion**

- ◦   Light sails use radiation pressure from photons to propel spacecraft. Advanced civilizations could build massive light sails powered by lasers or stellar energy.
- ◦   Breakthrough Starshot, a human-led initiative, aims to develop laser-driven light sails capable of reaching Alpha Centauri in 20 years (Parkin, 2018).

4.   **Antimatter Propulsion**

- ◦ Antimatter-matter annihilation produces immense amounts of energy, potentially allowing spacecraft to reach relativistic speeds.
- ◦ Antimatter propulsion remains speculative due to the difficulty of producing and storing sufficient quantities of antimatter. However, an advanced civilization might have solved these challenges (Forward, 1985).

5.   Generation Ships

- ◦ A slower approach involves spacecraft designed to sustain multiple generations of travelers over thousands of years. These "generation ships" would carry self-sustaining ecosystems and resources to ensure long-term survival.
- ◦ While feasible with human technology, this method may be less appealing for advanced civilizations capable of faster travel.

6.   Interdimensional Travel

- ◦ Some researchers suggest that extraterrestrials might utilize higher dimensions or parallel universes to bypass conventional spacetime constraints.
- ◦ L.A. Marzulli and other theorists propose that interdimensional travel might account for the sudden appearances and disappearances of UFOs, suggesting that advanced civilizations operate beyond our three-dimensional understanding (Marzulli, 2013).

Potential Energy Sources for Interstellar Travel

1.   Zero-Point Energy

- Zero-point energy, derived from quantum fluctuations in empty space, could provide a nearly limitless power source for advanced propulsion systems (Puthoff, 1990).
- If extraterrestrials have harnessed zero-point energy, it would enable technologies like warp drives and wormholes.

2.   Dyson Spheres

- A Dyson Sphere is a megastructure that surrounds a star to capture its energy output. Such a structure would provide an advanced civilization with the immense energy required for interstellar travel (Dyson, 1960).

3.   Fusion Reactors

- Fusion power, the process that powers stars, could serve as a practical energy source for long-distance space travel. Compact fusion reactors might allow spacecraft to sustain propulsion over decades or centuries.

Implications of Interstellar Travel for ETs

1. **Exploration and Colonization**

   ○ Extraterrestrial civilizations might explore other star systems to expand their knowledge, colonize habitable planets, or ensure the survival of their species.
   ○ Dr. Michael Salla speculates that interstellar travel could involve diplomatic missions, resource acquisition, or scientific research (Salla, 2004).

2. **Communication Challenges**

   ○ Even with advanced propulsion, interstellar travel involves delays in communication. Civilizations might develop autonomous probes or artificial intelligence to act as intermediaries.

3. **Cultural and Philosophical Motivations**

   ○ Advanced civilizations might view interstellar travel as a moral or spiritual imperative, seeking to share knowledge or connect with other intelligent species.

Insights from Key Figures

1. **Dr. Steven Greer**

○   Greer emphasizes that many UFO sightings suggest propulsion methods vastly superior to human technology. He argues that these sightings demonstrate practical examples of interstellar travel (Greer, 2017).

2.   **Dr. Michael Salla**

○   Salla envisions interstellar travel as a cornerstone of diplomatic engagement with extraterrestrial civilizations. He suggests that reverse-engineered technologies on Earth may one day enable humanity to participate in interstellar exploration (Salla, 2004).

3.   **L.A. Marzulli**

○   Marzulli links interstellar travel to spiritual dimensions, proposing that extraterrestrials might use advanced technology to traverse both physical and metaphysical realms (Marzulli, 2013).

Implications for Humanity

1.   **Technological Advancements**

○   Understanding extraterrestrial methods of interstellar travel could revolutionize human science, enabling humanity to explore beyond our solar system.

2. **Ethical Considerations**

   ◦ The pursuit of interstellar travel raises questions about humanity's responsibilities to other species and ecosystems, both on Earth and in space.

3. **A Broader Perspective**

   ◦ Learning from extraterrestrial civilizations would expand humanity's understanding of life, intelligence, and the universe, fostering a greater sense of unity and purpose.

Looking Ahead

Interstellar travel remains one of humanity's greatest aspirations and challenges. While current technology limits our reach, theoretical advancements and insights from UFO phenomena suggest that these limitations may not be insurmountable. By studying potential extraterrestrial methods of travel, humanity can prepare for a future where the stars are within reach.

Sources

1. Alcubierre, M. (1994). "The Warp Drive: Hyper-Fast Travel Within General Relativity." *Classical and Quantum Gravity*, 11(5), L73–L77.
2. Dyson, F. (1960). "Search for Artificial Stellar Sources of Infrared Radiation." *Science*, 131(3414), 1667–1668.

3. Forward, R. L. (1985). *Future Magic: How Today's Science Fiction Will Become Tomorrow's Reality*. Avon Books.

4. Greer, S. (2017). *Unacknowledged: An Exposé of the World's Greatest Secret*. A&M Publishing.

5. Lentz, E. W. (2021). "Breaking the Warp Barrier." *Classical and Quantum Gravity*, 38(7), 075015.

6. Marzulli, L. A. (2013). *The Watchers Series*. Spiral of Life.

7. NASA. (2023). "Interstellar Travel and the Challenges Ahead." Retrieved from nasa.gov.

8. Parkin, K. (2018). "The Breakthrough Starshot Program: A Feasibility Study." *Acta Astronautica*, 152, 370–377.

9. Puthoff, H. E. (1990). "Gravity as a Zero-Point-Fluctuation Force." *Physical Review A*, 39(5), 2333–2342.

10. Salla, M. (2004). *Exopolitics: Political Implications of the Extraterrestrial Presence*. Exopolitics Institute.

11. Thorne, K. S. (1994). *Black Holes and Time Warps: Einstein's Outrageous Legacy*. W.W. Norton & Company.

19

What Would They Want?

The motives of extraterrestrials visiting Earth could range from scientific curiosity to existential necessity. Understanding these possibilities is key to preparing for contact.
— Dr. Michio Kaku

The question of why extraterrestrial civilizations might visit Earth has intrigued scientists, philosophers, and researchers for decades. The possible reasons span a spectrum of motives, from scientific exploration to resource acquisition to spiritual or existential purposes. This chapter explores the various theories and perspectives on why aliens might be interested in Earth, drawing on scientific insights, historical patterns, and the work of prominent researchers like Dr. Steven Greer, Dr. Tom Horn, L.A. Marzulli, and Dr. Michael Salla.

1. Scientific Curiosity

1.   **Earth as a Biodiversity Hotspot**

     ◦   Earth's rich biodiversity and complex ecosystems could attract extraterrestrial scientists interested in studying the planet's life forms.

     ◦   Dr. Steven Greer suggests that advanced civilizations may view Earth as a "living laboratory," offering unique insights into the evolution of life in a diverse biosphere (Greer, 2017).

2.   **Observing Intelligent Life**

- Humanity's technological and cultural development might make Earth a point of interest for extraterrestrial anthropologists.
- The **Zoo Hypothesis** posits that extraterrestrials are observing Earth as part of a non-interference policy, similar to how humans study animals in the wild (Ball, 1973).

3.   **Shared Scientific Advancements**

- Contact with Earth could provide mutual benefits, as extraterrestrials might seek to exchange knowledge about science, technology, and the universe.

2. Resource Acquisition

1.   **Natural Resources**

- Earth's resources, such as water, minerals, and rare elements, might attract extraterrestrial visitors. For example, water is a valuable resource for sustaining life and producing hydrogen fuel.
- L.A. Marzulli suggests that the competition for resources could explain certain UFO sightings near industrial or natural resource sites (Marzulli, 2013).

2.   **Biological Resources**

- ◦ Some researchers speculate that extraterrestrials might be interested in Earth's genetic diversity.
- ◦ Alleged cases of alien abductions often describe experiments or genetic sampling, possibly indicating an interest in humanity's biology (Jacobs, 1998).

3.   **Energy Harvesting**

- ◦ Advanced civilizations may harvest energy from stars, planets, or other celestial bodies. Earth's proximity to the Sun and its natural resources might make it an ideal candidate for such activities.

3. Environmental and Planetary Stewardship

1.   **Protecting Earth's Ecosystems**

- ◦ Extraterrestrial civilizations might view Earth as a unique ecosystem worth preserving.
- ◦ UFO sightings near nuclear facilities and environmental hotspots suggest a possible concern about humanity's impact on the planet's stability (Hastings, 2010).

2.   **Preventing Catastrophe**

- Advanced civilizations might intervene to prevent humanity from self-destructive behaviors, such as nuclear warfare or ecological collapse.
- Dr. Michael Salla argues that extraterrestrials may see humanity as a developing species requiring guidance to avoid existential threats (Salla, 2004).

4. Cultural Exchange and Communication

1.   Sharing Knowledge and Culture

- Aliens might visit Earth to engage in cultural exchange, sharing their advancements in art, philosophy, and technology.
- Dr. Michio Kaku suggests that an advanced civilization might offer solutions to humanity's challenges, fostering a collaborative relationship (Kaku, 2018).

2.   Understanding Humanity's Potential

- Humanity's creativity, adaptability, and resilience might fascinate extraterrestrials, prompting them to observe or engage with us.

5. Spiritual and Existential Motives

1.   Exploring Consciousness

- Advanced extraterrestrial beings might seek to understand or share knowledge about consciousness and the nature of existence.
- Dr. Steven Greer proposes that some civilizations might operate on a higher plane of consciousness, emphasizing spiritual and metaphysical exploration (Greer, 2020).

2. **Spiritual Guidance or Manipulation**

- Dr. Tom Horn and L.A. Marzulli suggest that extraterrestrials might present themselves as spiritual beings or gods, influencing humanity's beliefs and practices. They caution against potential deception, drawing parallels to historical accounts of divine intervention (Horn & Putnam, 2013; Marzulli, 2013).

6. Galactic Politics and Alliances

1. **Diplomatic Engagement**

- Aliens might visit Earth as part of a diplomatic mission, establishing alliances or monitoring humanity's readiness for interstellar relations.
- Dr. Michael Salla, a proponent of exopolitics, theorizes that Earth could be integrated into a broader galactic community if humanity demonstrates maturity and cooperation (Salla, 2004).

2.   **Monitoring Potential Threats**

- ○   Humanity's rapid technological advancements, particularly in artificial intelligence and weaponry, might concern extraterrestrial civilizations.
- ○   They could view Earth as a potential threat or asset, warranting closer observation.

7. Existential Necessity

1.   **Survival and Relocation**

- ○   An extraterrestrial civilization might face existential threats, such as planetary collapse or resource depletion, prompting them to seek refuge or resources on Earth.
- ○   Stephen Hawking warned that humanity might face similar pressures in the future, necessitating interstellar expansion (Hawking, 2010).

2.   **Experimentation and Terraforming**

- ○   Aliens might experiment with terraforming or modifying Earth's environment to suit their needs, potentially reshaping the planet over time.

Ethical Implications

1. **Mutual Respect and Collaboration**

   ◦ Understanding extraterrestrial motives is essential to fostering respectful and mutually beneficial interactions.

2. **Safeguarding Humanity's Interests**

   ◦ Humanity must remain vigilant about potential exploitation or manipulation, ensuring that any engagement aligns with global ethical standards.

3. **The Role of Governments and Institutions**

   ◦ Transparent policies and international cooperation will be crucial in managing extraterrestrial contact and protecting humanity's sovereignty.

Looking Ahead

The reasons extraterrestrials might visit Earth reflect a wide range of possibilities, from scientific curiosity to existential necessity. By preparing for these scenarios and fostering a balanced approach, humanity can navigate the complexities of potential contact and ensure that such encounters contribute positively to our shared future.

Sources

1. Ball, J. A. (1973). "The Zoo Hypothesis." *Icarus*, 19(3), 347–349.

2. Greer, S. (2017). *Unacknowledged: An Exposé of the World's Greatest Secret*. A&M Publishing.

3. Greer, S. (2020). *Close Encounters of the Fifth Kind*. A&M Publishing.

4. Hastings, R. (2010). *UFOs and Nukes: Extraordinary Encounters at Nuclear Weapons Sites*. AuthorHouse.

5. Horn, T., & Putnam, C. (2013). *Exo-Vaticana: Petrus Romanus, Project Lucifer, and the Vatican's Astonishing Plan for the Arrival of an Alien Savior*. Defender Publishing.

6. Jacobs, D. M. (1998). *The Threat: Revealing the Secret Alien Agenda*. Simon & Schuster.

7. Kaku, M. (2018). *The Future of Humanity: Terraforming Mars, Interstellar Travel, Immortality, and Our Destiny Beyond Earth*. Doubleday.

8. Marzulli, L. A. (2013). *The Watchers Series*. Spiral of Life.

9. Salla, M. (2004). *Exopolitics: Political Implications of the Extraterrestrial Presence*. Exopolitics Institute.

Part IV: Humanity Transformed

20

The Religious Perspective

The discovery of extraterrestrial life would profoundly impact theology, challenging humanity to reconsider its understanding of God, creation, and the universe.
— Hugh Ross

The possibility of extraterrestrial life has long intrigued theologians and religious scholars. Different faiths approach the question from varied perspectives, with interpretations rooted in their doctrines and sacred texts. For Christianity, the Book of Enoch—a collection of ancient Jewish texts excluded from the biblical canon—plays a pivotal role in discussions about extraterrestrials, often associated with angels, Nephilim, and otherworldly beings. This chapter examines how major religions might interpret the existence of aliens, incorporating insights from scholars such as Brian Godawa, Jacques Vallée, Hugh Ross, and Ron Rhodes.

1. The Book of Enoch and Its Role in the Conversation

1. Overview of the Book of Enoch

- The Book of Enoch, a non-canonical Jewish text written around the 3rd century BC, describes interactions between humans and celestial beings called "Watchers."

- These Watchers, according to the text, descended to Earth, intermarried with human women, and produced the Nephilim—giants or hybrids with extraordinary abilities (1 Enoch 6–7).
- Many theologians and researchers, such as author Brian Godawa, interpret these accounts as evidence of divine or extraterrestrial intervention (Godawa, 2015).

2. Extraterrestrial Interpretations

- Some scholars suggest that the Watchers described in the Book of Enoch could be interpreted as extraterrestrial beings rather than traditional angels.
- Jacques Vallée, a UFO researcher, argues that many ancient texts, including the Book of Enoch, describe encounters with beings that resemble modern UFO and alien phenomena (Vallée, 1991).

3. Theological Implications

- If the Watchers are extraterrestrials, it raises questions about the nature of angels, demons, and their relationship to God.
- Ron Rhodes, in his work on biblical prophecy, cautions against conflating extraterrestrial entities with divine beings, emphasizing the need to discern between spiritual and physical phenomena (Rhodes, 2007).

2. Christianity and the Existence of Aliens

1. **Catholic Perspective**

   ○ The Vatican has publicly expressed openness to the existence of extraterrestrial life. Jesuit astronomer Guy Consolmagno stated that discovering aliens would not conflict with Catholic theology, as all creation is part of God's plan (Consolmagno, 2014).

   ○ Dr. Tom Horn and Cris Putnam, however, warn that the Vatican's stance might pave the way for theological reinterpretations that align extraterrestrial contact with end-times prophecy (Horn & Putnam, 2013).

2. **Evangelical Protestant Views**

   ○ Evangelicals like Ron Rhodes emphasize that the Bible focuses on humanity's relationship with God, leaving the existence of extraterrestrial life as an open question. Rhodes highlights that any alien contact must align with biblical teachings about creation and salvation (Rhodes, 2007).

3. **Hugh Ross's Astronomical Perspective**

   ○ Hugh Ross, a former Caltech astronomer, integrates science and theology, arguing that the rarity of Earth's conditions for life suggests that humanity holds a unique place in God's creation.

   ◦   Ross believes that reports of UFOs and extraterrestrial encounters may represent spiritual phenomena rather than physical beings (Ross, 2000).

3. Judaism and Islam

1.   Judaism

- Jewish theology, particularly Kabbalistic traditions, is open to the idea of multiple worlds created by God. The Zohar, a foundational text of Jewish mysticism, suggests that life could exist elsewhere in the universe.
- The Book of Enoch's description of celestial beings influencing human history aligns with interpretations of divine messengers in Jewish theology.

2.   Islam

- The Quran references the creation of other worlds, leaving room for the possibility of extraterrestrial life.
- Islamic scholars often interpret aliens as part of God's creation, emphasizing that they, like humans, are subject to divine will (Quran 42:29).

4. Eastern Religions

1.   Hinduism

- Hindu scriptures, such as the *Mahabharata* and *Ramayana*, describe vimanas—flying chariots used by gods and celestial beings.
- Some interpret these accounts as evidence of extraterrestrial technology, suggesting that Hindu cosmology inherently supports the idea of advanced beings visiting Earth (Childress, 2013).

2. **Buddhism**

- Buddhist teachings about the vastness of the universe and the existence of countless worlds align with the possibility of extraterrestrial life.
- The Dalai Lama has remarked that the discovery of alien life would be consistent with Buddhist philosophy, which emphasizes interconnectedness and the infinite nature of existence.

5. Key Research and Perspectives

1. **Jacques Vallée**

- Vallée's work, such as *Dimensions: A Casebook of Alien Contact*, examines the overlap between historical accounts of angels and modern UFO encounters. He suggests that these phenomena may represent the same entities observed through different cultural lenses (Vallée, 1991).

2.   **Brian Godawa**

- ◦   Godawa's research on the Nephilim connects ancient biblical accounts with modern UFO theories. He argues that the spiritual deception described in the Bible could manifest as extraterrestrial phenomena in contemporary times (Godawa, 2015).

3.   **Ron Rhodes**

- ◦   Rhodes emphasizes that Christians should interpret extraterrestrial encounters through a biblical framework, warning against accepting aliens as saviors or messianic figures (Rhodes, 2007).

4.   **Cornish College of the Arts Study**

- ◦   A study by Cornish College of the Arts analyzed the influence of extraterrestrial themes in art and religion, concluding that cultural depictions of aliens often reflect humanity's spiritual questions and aspirations (Cornish, 2019).

5.   **Hugh Ross**

- ◦   Ross integrates scientific evidence with theology, asserting that the absence of widespread extraterrestrial civilizations supports the biblical view of humanity's special role in creation (Ross, 2000).

6. Implications for Faith and Society

1. **Challenges to Traditional Beliefs**

   ○ The discovery of extraterrestrial life could challenge doctrines about humanity's uniqueness and the scope of salvation.
   ○ Religions would need to address questions about the spiritual status of aliens and their relationship to God.

2. **Opportunities for Unity**

   ○ Recognizing extraterrestrials as part of God's creation could foster interfaith dialogue and a deeper understanding of the universe's divine order.

3. **Spiritual Deception**

   ○ Some theologians caution that extraterrestrial phenomena could be used to mislead humanity, aligning with prophetic warnings about deception in the end times.

Looking Ahead

The religious interpretation of extraterrestrial life remains a dynamic and complex field. As humanity explores the cosmos, faith traditions will likely continue to evolve, incorporating new discoveries into their understanding of creation and existence. Whether viewed as divine messengers, spiritual entities, or advanced beings, extraterrestrials challenge humanity to expand its theological and philosophical horizons.

Sources

1. Childress, D. H. (2013). *Vimana: Aircraft of Ancient India & Atlantis*. Adventures Unlimited Press.

2. Consolmagno, G. (2014). *Would You Baptize an Extraterrestrial?*. Image.

3. Cornish College of the Arts. (2019). "Extraterrestrial Themes in Art and Religion: A Cultural Analysis." *Journal of Interdisciplinary Studies*.

4. Godawa, B. (2015). *When Giants Were Upon the Earth: The Watchers, Nephilim, and the Biblical Cosmic War of the Seed*. Embedded Pictures Publishing.

5. Horn, T., & Putnam, C. (2013). *Exo-Vaticana: Petrus Romanus, Project Lucifer, and the Vatican's Astonishing Plan for the Arrival of an Alien Savior*. Defender Publishing.

6. Rhodes, R. (2007). *Alien Obsession: What Lies Behind UFOs and the Coming Delusion*. Harvest House Publishers.

7. Ross, H. (2000). *Lights in the Sky and Little Green Men: A Rational Christian Look at UFOs and Extraterrestrials*. NavPress.

8. Vallée, J. (1991). *Dimensions: A Casebook of Alien Contact*. Ballantine Books.

21

Philosophical Implications

> **The question is not just whether extraterrestrial life exists, but what its existence would mean for humanity's understanding of itself and the universe.**
> — Dr. J. Allen Hynek

If extraterrestrial life exists, the implications extend beyond science and theology to the core of human philosophy. It forces us to rethink our place in the cosmos, our sense of purpose, and our understanding of consciousness, ethics, and reality itself. The work of key researchers like Dr. J. Allen Hynek, Stanton Friedman, Dr. John Mack, and Ann Druffel sheds light on these profound questions, providing insight into how contact with extraterrestrial life could redefine human identity and destiny.

1. Humanity's Place in the Universe

1. The Copernican Principle Extended

- The Copernican Revolution displaced humanity from the center of the universe. The discovery of extraterrestrial life would further challenge anthropocentrism by revealing that Earth is just one of countless planets hosting intelligent life.

○   Stanton Friedman, a nuclear physicist and UFO researcher, argued that accepting extraterrestrial life requires us to abandon the assumption that humanity occupies a privileged position in the cosmos (Friedman, 2008).

2.   Universal Consciousness

○   The possibility of extraterrestrial life raises questions about the nature of consciousness. Are humans unique in their capacity for self-awareness, or is consciousness a universal phenomenon?

○   Dr. John Mack, a Harvard psychiatrist, studied individuals who claimed to have experienced alien abductions. He argued that these experiences challenged conventional understandings of reality and consciousness, suggesting that extraterrestrial contact may involve expanded states of awareness (Mack, 1994).

2. Ethical and Moral Considerations

1.   Interstellar Morality

○   Contact with extraterrestrial civilizations would require humanity to develop new ethical frameworks for interstellar diplomacy and coexistence.

○   Ann Druffel, an expert in UFO encounters, emphasized that humanity must approach such contact with humility and an ethical commitment to peace and mutual understanding (Druffel, 1998).

2. **The Responsibility of Advanced Civilizations**

- ◦ If extraterrestrial civilizations possess advanced technology and knowledge, they might face ethical dilemmas about intervening in human affairs.
- ◦ Dr. J. Allen Hynek, a renowned astronomer and ufologist, suggested that extraterrestrial visitors might practice non-intervention, akin to the Prime Directive in *Star Trek*, due to ethical considerations about interfering with less advanced species (Hynek, 1972).

3. **Human Responsibility to the Cosmos**

- ◦ The awareness of extraterrestrial life might encourage humanity to take greater responsibility for preserving Earth's environment and promoting peace. The understanding that we are part of a larger cosmic community could foster global unity and cooperation.

3. The Nature of Reality

1. **Dimensions and Perception**

- ◦ Dr. John Mack argued that alien encounters challenge the materialist view of reality. He suggested that these experiences might represent interactions with beings from other dimensions or parallel realities (Mack, 1994).

- ° Ann Druffel's research on anomalous phenomena suggests that human perception might be limited by our five senses and that extraterrestrial life could operate in realms beyond our current understanding (Druffel, 1998).

2. The Role of Belief and Skepticism

- ° Dr. J. Allen Hynek shifted from a skeptic to a proponent of serious UFO research after investigating numerous credible cases as part of Project Blue Book. He argued that dismissing the possibility of extraterrestrial life without investigation reflects a failure of scientific curiosity (Hynek, 1972).
- ° Stanton Friedman criticized the scientific community's reluctance to study UFO phenomena, stating that true scientific inquiry demands open-mindedness and rigorous investigation (Friedman, 2008).

4. Existential and Spiritual Reflections

1. Humanity's Place in Cosmic Time

- ° The discovery of advanced extraterrestrial civilizations would raise questions about humanity's developmental stage in cosmic time. Are we an early species, destined to evolve further, or a latecomer in a universe already filled with advanced life?
- ° Stanton Friedman argued that extraterrestrial civilizations might be millions of years more advanced than hu-

manity, making us akin to primitive beings in comparison (Friedman, 2008).

2. **The Search for Meaning**

- ○ Dr. John Mack suggested that extraterrestrial contact could lead humanity to a spiritual awakening, challenging us to explore the deeper meaning of existence and our connection to the cosmos (Mack, 1994).

3. **The Fear of the Unknown**

- ○ Ann Druffel emphasized the psychological impact of encountering beings vastly different from ourselves. She noted that fear of the unknown is a fundamental human response but that overcoming this fear is essential for meaningful contact (Druffel, 1998).

5. The Role of Art and Philosophy

1. **Artistic Interpretation of Alien Contact**

- ○ Throughout history, artists and writers have explored the philosophical implications of extraterrestrial life, from H.G. Wells' *The War of the Worlds* to contemporary films like *Arrival*.

- ◦ These works encourage reflection on human nature, ethics, and the meaning of life in a vast and mysterious universe.

2. **Philosophical Paradigms**

- ◦ Philosophers like Immanuel Kant and Arthur Schopenhauer have long pondered the nature of existence and the possibility of life beyond Earth. The discovery of extraterrestrial civilizations would necessitate a reexamination of these philosophical paradigms.

6. Insights from Key Figures

1. **Dr. J. Allen Hynek**

- ◦ Hynek's transformation from a skeptic to a proponent of UFO research highlights the importance of remaining open to new evidence. He believed that the study of extraterrestrial phenomena could revolutionize human understanding of the universe (Hynek, 1972).

2. **Stanton Friedman**

- ◦ Friedman's work emphasized the need for rigorous scientific inquiry into UFO phenomena and criticized the scientific community's tendency to dismiss such research without investigation (Friedman, 2008).

3.　**Dr. John Mack**

○　Mack's research on alien abduction experiences challenged the materialist view of reality and suggested that extraterrestrial contact might involve expanded states of consciousness (Mack, 1994).

4.　**Ann Druffel**

○　Druffel's research emphasized the ethical and psychological challenges of extraterrestrial contact and the need for humanity to approach such encounters with humility and ethical responsibility (Druffel, 1998).

Looking Ahead

The philosophical implications of extraterrestrial life extend beyond the immediate scientific discovery of new species. They challenge us to reconsider our place in the universe, our understanding of reality, and our ethical responsibilities as a species. Whether extraterrestrial life represents a mirror, a teacher, or a challenge, its discovery would mark a transformative moment in human history.

Sources

1. Druffel, A. (1998). *How to Defend Yourself Against Alien Abduction*. Harmony Books.
2. Friedman, S. (2008). *Flying Saucers and Science: A Scientist Investigates the Mysteries of UFOs*. New Page Books.
3. Hynek, J. A. (1972). *The UFO Experience: A Scientific Inquiry*. Ballantine Books.
4. Mack, J. E. (1994). *Abduction: Human Encounters with Aliens*. Scribner.

22

Economic and Political Impacts

The discovery of extraterrestrial life and the introduction of free energy technology could upend every aspect of the global economic and political order.
— Dr. Steven Greer

The discovery of extraterrestrial civilizations and their advanced technologies would have profound implications for Earth's economic and political systems. Among the most transformative possibilities is the implementation of free energy technology, which could solve humanity's energy crisis but also destabilize entrenched power structures. This chapter explores the potential economic and political impacts of such a discovery, incorporating insights from researchers and experts like Dr. Steven Greer, Stanton Friedman, and Jacques Vallée.

1. The Potential of Free Energy Technology

1. **What Is Free Energy?**

   ° Free energy refers to limitless, clean energy derived from advanced technologies such as zero-point energy or vacuum energy. These concepts are rooted in quantum field theory, where energy is extracted from the vacuum of space (Puthoff, 1990).

○ Extraterrestrial civilizations, if advanced enough to traverse interstellar distances, may have already harnessed such technologies.

2. **Dr. Steven Greer's Advocacy**

○ Dr. Greer, in *Unacknowledged* (2017), argues that many UFO sightings involve craft powered by advanced energy systems. He believes these technologies are already within human reach, suppressed by governments and corporations to protect existing energy monopolies.

3. **Potential Benefits of Free Energy**

○ Free energy could eliminate reliance on fossil fuels, drastically reducing carbon emissions and mitigating climate change.
○ It could provide affordable energy to impoverished regions, promoting economic equality and improving quality of life globally.

2. Economic Implications

1. **Disruption of Energy Markets**

○ The global energy sector, valued at trillions of dollars, would face catastrophic disruption. Fossil fuel industries, including oil, coal, and natural gas, would become obsolete.

○   Nations reliant on energy exports, such as Saudi Arabia and Russia, would experience severe economic crises.

2.   **New Industries and Technologies**

○   Free energy could spur innovation in sectors such as transportation, manufacturing, and space exploration.

○   Industries focusing on traditional energy production and distribution would be replaced by those centered around advanced technologies, such as anti-gravity propulsion systems and zero-point energy generators.

3.   **Wealth Redistribution**

○   Access to free energy would reduce costs for individuals and businesses, potentially narrowing the wealth gap.

○   However, the transition could create significant economic instability, particularly for those heavily invested in outdated energy infrastructure.

4.   **Job Market Transformation**

○   Millions of jobs in the fossil fuel industry would disappear, necessitating large-scale workforce retraining programs.

- ° Simultaneously, new jobs would emerge in fields like quantum energy research, engineering, and advanced manufacturing.

3. Political Implications

1. Shift in Global Power Dynamics

- ° Nations controlling advanced energy technologies would gain significant geopolitical advantages.
- ° Developing nations with access to free energy could rapidly industrialize, challenging traditional power hierarchies.

2. Military Applications

- ° Free energy technologies could revolutionize defense systems, enabling the development of weapons and vehicles with unprecedented capabilities.
- ° Jacques Vallée warned that the militarization of extraterrestrial technology could escalate global conflicts if not carefully managed (Vallée, 1991).

3. Transparency and Governance

- ° The release of suppressed technologies would demand global transparency and collaboration. Dr. Greer advocates for international oversight to ensure equitable access to advanced energy systems (Greer, 2017).

- Governments may face public backlash for decades of secrecy surrounding UFOs and advanced technologies.

4. Social and Environmental Impacts

1.   Global Collaboration

- The introduction of free energy could encourage nations to work together on shared challenges, such as climate change and poverty.
- Conversely, competition over control of advanced technologies could exacerbate tensions between nations.

2.   Environmental Restoration

- The elimination of fossil fuels would reduce pollution, allowing ecosystems to recover and potentially reversing some effects of climate change.
- Access to clean energy would enable large-scale projects, such as desalination plants to combat water scarcity and reforestation efforts.

3.   Cultural Shifts

- ○ Societies might shift from consumer-driven economies to those focused on sustainability and innovation.
- ○ The discovery of extraterrestrial civilizations could inspire a broader sense of global unity, encouraging humanity to prioritize long-term survival over short-term profits.

5. Challenges to Implementation

1. Resistance from Established Powers

- ○ Corporations and governments with vested interests in the energy sector may resist the adoption of free energy technologies, fearing economic and political losses.
- ○ Stanton Friedman argued that secrecy around UFOs and advanced technologies is driven by a desire to maintain control over existing power structures (Friedman, 2008).

2. Technological Hurdles

- ○ Reverse-engineering extraterrestrial technologies would require significant scientific advancements and international collaboration.
- ○ Ensuring safe and equitable distribution of these technologies would present logistical challenges.

3. Ethical Considerations

- Who should control free energy technology? How can it be distributed equitably? These questions would require the creation of new ethical frameworks and governance systems.

6. Insights from Key Figures

1. **Dr. Steven Greer**

   - Greer emphasizes that the release of advanced technologies could solve global crises but warns that secrecy and militarization could hinder progress (Greer, 2017).

2. **Jacques Vallée**

   - Vallée cautions that the introduction of extraterrestrial technologies could destabilize existing systems if not carefully managed. He advocates for transparency and scientific rigor in studying these technologies (Vallée, 1991).

3. **Stanton Friedman**

   - Friedman argued that UFO secrecy is driven by economic and political interests, with powerful entities fearing the transformative impact of free energy and advanced technologies (Friedman, 2008).

Looking Ahead

The implementation of free energy and the discovery of extraterrestrial civilizations could mark the dawn of a new era for humanity, with opportunities to address global challenges and achieve unprecedented progress. However, realizing this potential will require careful planning, ethical governance, and global cooperation to ensure that these advancements benefit all of humanity rather than a select few.

Sources

1.   Friedman, S. (2008). *Flying Saucers and Science: A Scientist Investigates the Mysteries of UFOs*. New Page Books.

2.   Greer, S. (2017). *Unacknowledged: An Exposé of the World's Greatest Secret*. A&M Publishing.

3.   Puthoff, H. E. (1990). "Gravity as a Zero-Point-Fluctuation Force." *Physical Review A*, 39(5), 2333–2342.

4.   Vallée, J. (1991). *Dimensions: A Casebook of Alien Contact*. Ballantine Books.

23

The Psychological Effect

> The discovery of alien life would profoundly alter humanity's perception of itself, challenging deeply held beliefs and reshaping our collective consciousness.
> — Dr. John E. Mack

The confirmation of extraterrestrial life would be one of the most transformative events in human history, fundamentally altering our understanding of existence, purpose, and place in the universe. While the scientific, religious, and cultural implications are often discussed, the psychological effects of such a discovery are equally significant. This chapter examines how individuals and societies might cope with the knowledge of alien life, incorporating insights from researchers like Dr. John E. Mack, Ann Druffel, Carl Jung, and others.

1. Individual Psychological Reactions

1. Shock and Disbelief

- Initial reactions to the discovery of alien life are likely to include disbelief, fear, and cognitive dissonance.
- Dr. John Mack, who studied individuals claiming alien abductions, observed that many experienced intense psychological upheaval, ranging from denial to existential crises (Mack, 1994).

2. **Fear of the Unknown**

- The prospect of encountering beings vastly different from humans could trigger primal fears of the unknown.
- Ann Druffel noted that many UFO witnesses report feelings of powerlessness and vulnerability, which can lead to long-term anxiety or PTSD-like symptoms (Druffel, 1998).

3. **Curiosity and Wonder**

- For others, the discovery of alien life might inspire awe and curiosity, encouraging exploration and a broader understanding of the universe.
- Carl Jung, in *Flying Saucers: A Modern Myth of Things Seen in the Skies*, argued that UFO phenomena often evoke archetypal responses, tapping into humanity's collective unconscious and yearning for connection with the cosmos (Jung, 1959).

2. Societal Reactions

1. Cultural and Religious Upheaval

- The confirmation of alien life would challenge many cultural and religious narratives, potentially leading to widespread reevaluation of core beliefs.

○ Carl Sagan noted that humanity might initially struggle to reconcile extraterrestrial life with anthropocentric worldviews but ultimately adapt to this expanded perspective (Sagan, 1994).

2. **Misinformation and Panic**

○ Misinformation and fear-based narratives could exacerbate public anxiety.

○ Dr. Steven Greer has warned that governments might exploit public fear of extraterrestrials to maintain control or justify militarization (Greer, 2017).

3. **Social Polarization**

○ Societal reactions could vary widely, with some embracing the discovery as an opportunity for growth and others resisting it due to fear or mistrust.

○ This polarization could lead to divisions between those who accept the reality of extraterrestrial life and those who reject it.

3. Psychological Models for Understanding

1. **Kubler-Ross Model of Grief**

- The psychological adjustment to alien life might mirror the stages of grief: denial, anger, bargaining, depression, and acceptance.
- Ann Druffel suggested that individuals experiencing UFO-related trauma often undergo similar emotional processes before reaching acceptance (Druffel, 1998).

2.   **Maslow's Hierarchy of Needs**

- The confirmation of alien life could impact humanity's sense of safety, belonging, and self-actualization.
- Dr. John Mack argued that the discovery might push humanity toward the top of Maslow's hierarchy, encouraging existential and spiritual exploration (Mack, 1994).

4. Long-Term Impacts on Human Psychology

1.   **Expansion of Worldviews**

- The realization that humanity is not alone in the universe could lead to a shift from an Earth-centric perspective to a cosmic perspective.
- Carl Sagan envisioned a future where humanity's sense of identity expands to include its role as a member of a galactic community (Sagan, 1994).

2.   **Collective Trauma or Growth**

- The psychological impact of discovering alien life would depend on the circumstances of the discovery.

  - A peaceful encounter might foster unity and curiosity.
  - A hostile or ambiguous encounter could lead to widespread fear and trauma.

3. **Enhanced Resilience**

- Over time, humanity's ability to adapt to new realities could strengthen, fostering resilience and a broader sense of interconnectedness.

5. Insights from Key Figures

1. **Dr. John E. Mack**

- Mack's research on alien abduction experiences revealed that many individuals eventually viewed their encounters as transformative, leading to greater spiritual awareness and personal growth (Mack, 1994).

2. **Ann Druffel**

- Druffel emphasized the importance of psychological preparation for alien contact, advocating for mental resilience and emotional processing to prevent long-term distress (Druffel, 1998).

3.   Carl Jung

- Jung viewed UFO phenomena as symbols of humanity's collective unconscious, reflecting deeper archetypal fears and aspirations. He argued that understanding these symbols could help individuals integrate the discovery of alien life into their psychological frameworks (Jung, 1959).

4.   Carl Sagan

- Sagan championed the idea that humanity's psychological response to alien life would evolve over time, shifting from fear and disbelief to acceptance and wonder (Sagan, 1994).

6. Preparing for the Psychological Effects

1.   Education and Public Awareness

- Governments and institutions should educate the public about the possibilities of extraterrestrial life, fostering curiosity and reducing fear.

2.   **Mental Health Support**

- ◦ Psychological support systems, including counseling and therapy, would be essential to help individuals and communities cope with the discovery.

3.   **Promoting Unity and Collaboration**

- ◦ Emphasizing humanity's shared identity and collective future could mitigate divisive reactions and promote a sense of global unity.

Looking Ahead

The psychological effects of discovering alien life would be as profound as they are varied. While fear and uncertainty would likely dominate initial reactions, humanity's innate curiosity and adaptability could ultimately lead to growth and transformation. By preparing for these possibilities, humanity can ensure a smoother transition to a new understanding of its place in the universe.

Sources

1.   Druffel, A. (1998). *How to Defend Yourself Against Alien Abduction*. Harmony Books.
2.   Greer, S. (2017). *Unacknowledged: An Exposé of the World's Greatest Secret*. A&M Publishing.
3.   Jung, C. G. (1959). *Flying Saucers: A Modern Myth of Things Seen in the Skies*. Harcourt Brace.

4.   Mack, J. E. (1994). *Abduction: Human Encounters with Aliens*. Scribner.

5.   Sagan, C. (1994). *Pale Blue Dot: A Vision of the Human Future in Space*. Random House.

24

Communication Challenges

**If we ever come face to face with extraterrestrial intelli-
gence, our greatest challenge may not be making contact,
but understanding what they're saying.**
— Dr. Douglas Vakoch

Effective communication with extraterrestrial civilizations would be one of humanity's most complex and profound challenges. The barriers of language, culture, cognition, and even physical senses could make it extraordinarily difficult to understand or be understood by alien species. This chapter explores potential communication challenges and strategies for overcoming them, drawing on research from Dr. Douglas Vakoch, Carl Sagan, Dr. John C. Lilly, and others.

1. Barriers to Communication

1. Differences in Cognition and Perception

- Extraterrestrials may have entirely different sensory systems and cognitive frameworks, perceiving the universe in ways humans cannot comprehend.
- Dr. John C. Lilly, in his work on interspecies communication, emphasized that non-human intelligence might operate on vastly different planes of consciousness (Lilly, 1967).

2. **Language Incompatibility**

   ○   Human languages are based on shared experiences and environments, which aliens may not possess. Concepts like time, space, or emotion might be expressed—or absent—in entirely different ways.

3. **Symbolic Representation**

   ○   Aliens might communicate using symbols, mathematics, or visual patterns instead of verbal language. Decoding these symbols would require identifying their underlying logic.

4. **Temporal and Technological Gaps**

   ○   Advanced civilizations might use forms of communication beyond human comprehension, such as quantum entanglement or higher-dimensional signals.

2. Lessons from Human and Interspecies Communication

1. **Human Linguistic Diversity**

- ◦   The study of human languages, including translation and code-breaking, offers insights into how to approach alien communication.
- ◦   The Rosetta Stone, which helped decode Egyptian hieroglyphs, illustrates the importance of finding common references in communication.

2.   Interspecies Communication

- ◦   Research on communicating with dolphins, primates, and other animals reveals the challenges of understanding non-human intelligence.
- ◦   Dr. John C. Lilly's work with dolphins demonstrated that understanding their communication required patience, empathy, and innovative thinking (Lilly, 1967).

3. Strategies for Overcoming Communication Barriers

1.   Mathematics as a Universal Language

- ◦   Mathematics is often considered a universal language because its principles are consistent throughout the universe.
- ◦   Carl Sagan's *Contact* (1985) explores how mathematics might be used as a common framework for communication with extraterrestrial civilizations.
- ◦   The Arecibo Message, transmitted in 1974, used binary-coded data to represent basic concepts such as num-

bers, chemical elements, and human biology (Sagan, 1974).

2. **Non-Verbal Communication**

- Visual symbols, patterns, and imagery could serve as a bridge between human and alien communication systems.
- NASA's Voyager Golden Records, launched in 1977, include images, music, and greetings in multiple languages to provide a snapshot of humanity's culture and environment (Lomberg, 1978).

3. **AI and Machine Learning**

- Artificial intelligence could play a crucial role in decoding alien languages by identifying patterns and correlations in large data sets.
- Dr. Douglas Vakoch emphasizes the importance of using AI to process and interpret extraterrestrial signals, as human cognition may not be equipped to handle the complexity of alien communication (Vakoch, 2014).

4. **Shared Context**

- Establishing common ground is essential for effective communication. This could involve using universal physical phenomena, such as the properties of hydrogen or the periodic table of elements, as a starting point.

4. Challenges in Real-Time Communication

1.   Delay in Signal Exchange

- Signals traveling at the speed of light would take years, decades, or even centuries to travel between Earth and distant civilizations.
- This delay would make real-time communication impossible, requiring patience and long-term commitment.

2.   Misinterpretation

- Without a shared cultural or cognitive framework, messages could be misinterpreted, leading to unintended consequences.
- The Fermi Paradox highlights the risks of misunderstanding alien intentions, emphasizing the need for caution in initial communications (Hart, 1975).

5. Case Studies of Communication Attempts

1.   The Pioneer Plaques (1972–1973)

- ◦ Designed by Carl Sagan and Frank Drake, the plaques aboard the Pioneer spacecraft included pictorial messages representing human anatomy, Earth's location, and the solar system.
- ◦ While the simplicity of the plaques ensures clarity, their reliance on human-centric symbols may limit their effectiveness for alien interpretation (Sagan, 1972).

2. **The Arecibo Message (1974)**

- ◦ Transmitted toward the M13 star cluster, the Arecibo Message encoded information about human biology, the solar system, and Earth's inhabitants.
- ◦ Its mathematical and binary structure was designed to appeal to universally recognizable patterns (Sagan, 1974).

3. **Breakthrough Listen (2015–Present)**

- ◦ This initiative involves scanning the skies for extraterrestrial signals and preparing for potential communication.
- ◦ The program employs cutting-edge technology and AI to analyze vast amounts of data for patterns that could indicate intelligent design (Worden, 2016).

6. Insights from Key Figures

1. **Dr. Douglas Vakoch**

    °   Vakoch, a leader in METI (Messaging Extraterrestrial Intelligence), advocates for proactive communication efforts. He emphasizes the importance of preparing humanity for the ethical and philosophical challenges of contact (Vakoch, 2014).

2.   **Carl Sagan**

    °   Sagan's work highlights the importance of humility and curiosity in communicating with extraterrestrials. He believed that establishing common ground through science and mathematics was humanity's best chance for meaningful dialogue (Sagan, 1994).

3.   **Dr. John C. Lilly**

    °   Lilly's research on dolphin communication underscores the importance of flexibility and creativity in understanding non-human intelligence. His work suggests that open-mindedness is key to interpreting alien communication (Lilly, 1967).

Looking Ahead

Effective communication with extraterrestrial civilizations would require a multidisciplinary approach, combining linguistics, mathematics, artificial intelligence, and creativity. Preparing for this challenge is not just a scientific endeavor but a philosophical and cultural one, demanding that humanity confront its assumptions about language, intelligence, and connection.

Sources

1. Hart, M. H. (1975). "An Explanation for the Absence of Extraterrestrials on Earth." *Quarterly Journal of the Royal Astronomical Society*, 16, 128–135.

2. Lilly, J. C. (1967). *Man and Dolphin: Adventures on a New Scientific Frontier*. Doubleday.

3. Lomberg, J. (1978). "The Voyager Record: A Tool for Interstellar Communication." *Science*, 199(4332), 872–876.

4. Sagan, C. (1972). *The Pioneer Plaque: Humanity's First Interstellar Message*. NASA.

5. Sagan, C. (1974). "The Arecibo Message." *Science*, 186(4168), 920–926.

6. Sagan, C. (1994). *Pale Blue Dot: A Vision of the Human Future in Space*. Random House.

7. Vakoch, D. A. (2014). *Extraterrestrial Altruism: Evolution and Ethics in the Cosmos*. Springer.

8. Worden, P., et al. (2016). "Breakthrough Listen: A New Search for ET." *Publications of the Astronomical Society of the Pacific*, 128(959).

25

Global Cooperation or Conflict?

The discovery of extraterrestrial life may either unify humanity under a shared purpose or exacerbate existing divisions, depending on how we choose to respond.
— Carl Sagan

The confirmation of extraterrestrial life would undoubtedly transform global politics, potentially serving as a catalyst for unprecedented cooperation—or conflict. Whether humanity unites to address the challenges and opportunities of contact or fractures under the weight of fear and competition depends on the choices made by governments, institutions, and individuals. This chapter explores the scenarios under which alien discovery could either unify or divide humanity, drawing on insights from Carl Sagan, Dr. Steven Greer, Jacques Vallée, and other scholars.

1. The Potential for Global Unity

1. A Shared Existential Moment

- The realization that humanity is not alone in the universe could foster a sense of collective identity, transcending national, cultural, and religious boundaries.
- Carl Sagan posited that the discovery of extraterrestrial life could create a "cosmic perspective," encouraging hu-

manity to view Earth as a single entity in the vast expanse of space (Sagan, 1994).

2.   **Collaborative Problem-Solving**

- ◦   Addressing the challenges of alien contact, such as communication, ethical considerations, and resource management, would require international collaboration.
- ◦   The Outer Space Treaty of 1967, which emphasizes the peaceful exploration of space, provides a framework for such cooperation (UNOOSA, 1967).

3.   **Inspiration for Scientific Progress**

- ◦   Discovering advanced extraterrestrial technology could inspire global investment in science, technology, and education, fostering a new era of innovation and discovery.
- ◦   Dr. Steven Greer argues that transparency in sharing extraterrestrial technologies could eliminate global inequities and promote sustainable development (Greer, 2017).

2. Risks of Division and Conflict

1.   **Resource Competition**

- ○ Nations or corporations might compete for access to extraterrestrial knowledge, technology, or potential resources, leading to geopolitical tensions.
- ○ Jacques Vallée warns that the militarization of extraterrestrial discoveries could exacerbate global conflicts rather than resolve them (Vallée, 1991).

2.   Mistrust and Fear

- ○ Fear of the unknown could lead to xenophobia, misinformation, and panic, as nations struggle to control the narrative around extraterrestrial contact.
- ○ Dr. Steven Greer has expressed concerns about governments using extraterrestrial discoveries to justify military spending and authoritarian policies (Greer, 2017).

3.   Unequal Access to Technology

- ○ If extraterrestrial technologies are monopolized by powerful nations or corporations, existing global inequalities could worsen, leading to resentment and unrest.
- ○ Dr. Michael Salla advocates for the equitable distribution of alien-derived technologies to prevent economic and political imbalances (Salla, 2004).

3. Historical Parallels and Lessons

1. The Cold War Space Race

- The space race of the mid-20th century demonstrated how technological competition can both drive innovation and fuel geopolitical rivalry.
- Similar dynamics could emerge if extraterrestrial technology becomes a new frontier of competition.

2. Colonialism and Indigenous Encounters

- Historical encounters between technologically advanced societies and less advanced ones often led to exploitation and suffering.
- Stanton Friedman warned that humanity must avoid replicating these patterns if extraterrestrial civilizations engage with Earth (Friedman, 2008).

3. Global Responses to Shared Threats

- The COVID-19 pandemic highlighted both the potential for global cooperation and the challenges of achieving it in the face of a shared crisis.
- These lessons underscore the importance of transparent communication and equitable resource distribution in responding to extraterrestrial contact.

4. The Role of International Organizations

1. **United Nations**

   - The United Nations Office for Outer Space Affairs (UNOOSA) could play a central role in coordinating global responses to extraterrestrial contact, building on frameworks like the Outer Space Treaty.
   - However, the UN's effectiveness would depend on the willingness of member states to cooperate and share information.

2. **Scientific Communities**

   - Organizations like the International Astronomical Union and SETI (Search for Extraterrestrial Intelligence) could provide scientific leadership, ensuring that responses are guided by evidence and expertise.
   - Collaborative research initiatives, similar to the Large Hadron Collider project, could foster international partnerships.

3. **Non-Governmental Organizations (NGOs)**

   - NGOs focused on ethics, human rights, and environmental sustainability could advocate for equitable and peaceful approaches to extraterrestrial contact.

5. Ethical Considerations

1. **Transparency and Accountability**

   - Governments and institutions must prioritize transparency in sharing information about extraterrestrial discoveries to build public trust and prevent misinformation.
   - Carl Sagan emphasized the importance of open dialogue and public engagement in addressing questions of cosmic significance (Sagan, 1994).

2. **Avoiding Militarization**

   - The potential weaponization of extraterrestrial technologies poses significant ethical and existential risks.
   - Jacques Vallée and others advocate for strict international agreements to prevent the use of alien technologies for destructive purposes (Vallée, 1991).

3. **Equitable Access**

   - Ensuring that all nations and communities benefit from extraterrestrial discoveries is critical to fostering global unity and preventing resentment.

6. Insights from Key Figures

1. **Carl Sagan**

   ◦ Sagan believed that the discovery of extraterrestrial life could inspire a sense of global unity, encouraging humanity to confront shared challenges with a renewed perspective (Sagan, 1994).

2. **Dr. Steven Greer**

   ◦ Greer advocates for the disclosure of suppressed technologies and the development of peaceful, collaborative approaches to extraterrestrial contact (Greer, 2017).

3. **Jacques Vallée**

   ◦ Vallée warns that competition and secrecy could undermine humanity's ability to respond effectively to extraterrestrial contact, emphasizing the need for transparency and ethical governance (Vallée, 1991).

4. **Stanton Friedman**

   ◦ Friedman highlighted the risks of militarizing extraterrestrial discoveries, urging humanity to approach the issue with humility and caution (Friedman, 2008).

Looking Ahead

The discovery of extraterrestrial life could serve as either a unifying force or a source of conflict, depending on humanity's response. By prioritizing transparency, collaboration, and ethical decision-making, we can ensure that this transformative event contributes to a more unified and equitable global society.

Sources

1. Friedman, S. (2008). *Flying Saucers and Science: A Scientist Investigates the Mysteries of UFOs*. New Page Books.
2. Greer, S. (2017). *Unacknowledged: An Exposé of the World's Greatest Secret*. A&M Publishing.
3. Sagan, C. (1994). *Pale Blue Dot: A Vision of the Human Future in Space*. Random House.
4. Salla, M. (2004). *Exopolitics: Political Implications of the Extraterrestrial Presence*. Exopolitics Institute.
5. UNOOSA. (1967). *The Outer Space Treaty*. United Nations Office for Outer Space Affairs.
6. Vallée, J. (1991). *Dimensions: A Casebook of Alien Contact*. Ballantine Books.

26

Scientific Revolution

The discovery of alien knowledge would represent the greatest leap in human understanding since the scientific revolution, fundamentally reshaping our view of the universe and our place within it.
— Carl Sagan

Contact with extraterrestrial intelligence and the acquisition of their knowledge could spark a scientific revolution unparalleled in human history. Advanced alien civilizations might possess insights into physics, biology, medicine, and energy that could accelerate humanity's progress by centuries or millennia. This chapter explores how alien knowledge might transform human understanding, incorporating insights from Carl Sagan, Dr. Michio Kaku, Dr. Steven Greer, and other prominent thinkers.

1. Physics and Cosmology

1. Unified Theories of Physics

- Humanity's quest for a unified theory of physics—integrating quantum mechanics and general relativity—might be resolved through alien knowledge.
- Dr. Michio Kaku theorizes that advanced civilizations would have already achieved this synthesis, potentially un-

locking new dimensions of spacetime and revolutionizing our understanding of the cosmos (Kaku, 2008).

2.   **Advanced Propulsion Systems**

- Alien civilizations capable of interstellar travel would likely use propulsion systems that far exceed human technology, such as warp drives or wormholes.
- Miguel Alcubierre's theoretical model of a warp drive, which manipulates spacetime, could become a reality with insights from extraterrestrial physics (Alcubierre, 1994).

3.   **Dark Matter and Dark Energy**

- Extraterrestrial knowledge might shed light on the nature of dark matter and dark energy, which together comprise 95% of the universe's mass-energy content but remain poorly understood.

2. Energy and Sustainability

1.   **Zero-Point Energy**

- Theoretical zero-point energy, derived from quantum vacuum fluctuations, could provide a limitless, clean energy source.

○ Dr. Steven Greer has argued that extraterrestrial civilizations likely harness this energy, enabling advanced propulsion and sustainable societies (Greer, 2017).

2. **Dyson Spheres and Energy Harvesting**

○ Advanced civilizations may construct megastructures like Dyson Spheres to capture a star's energy output. Such technology could revolutionize human energy systems, eliminating reliance on fossil fuels (Dyson, 1960).

3. **Revolutionizing Sustainability**

○ Access to extraterrestrial energy technologies could enable large-scale environmental restoration, desalination, and agricultural innovation, addressing global challenges like climate change and resource scarcity.

3. Medicine and Biotechnology

1. **Advanced Medical Technologies**

○ Alien civilizations may possess knowledge of diseases, genetic engineering, and regenerative medicine far beyond human capabilities.

    °   Techniques like molecular nanotechnology could allow for cell-by-cell repair of tissues, effectively curing aging and many diseases (Freitas, 1999).

2.   Understanding Consciousness

    °   Extraterrestrials might offer insights into the biological and quantum basis of consciousness, transforming fields like neuroscience and psychology.

    °   Dr. John Mack suggested that alien contact experiences often involve expanded states of awareness, hinting at a deeper understanding of consciousness among advanced beings (Mack, 1994).

3.   Eradicating Disease

    °   Knowledge of alien biology could provide breakthroughs in immunology and virology, enabling the eradication of diseases that have plagued humanity for centuries.

4. Computing and Artificial Intelligence

1.   Quantum Computing

- Alien civilizations may have mastered quantum computing, allowing for exponentially faster data processing and problem-solving.
- This could lead to breakthroughs in fields ranging from climate modeling to cryptography and materials science.

2. **Artificial General Intelligence (AGI)**

- Insights into extraterrestrial artificial intelligence could help humanity develop AGI systems capable of reasoning and learning like humans—or beyond.
- Ethical considerations would be paramount, as AGI could dramatically alter the dynamics of human society and labor.

5. Social Sciences and Philosophy

1. **Understanding Civilization Dynamics**

- Studying alien civilizations could provide valuable insights into how societies evolve, avoid self-destruction, and sustain long-term stability.
- Dr. Michio Kaku's *The Physics of the Future* emphasizes that civilizations capable of interstellar travel have likely overcome significant social and environmental challenges (Kaku, 2011).

2.   **Cosmic Ethics**

- Alien knowledge might introduce new ethical frameworks for interstellar relations, resource use, and the treatment of other species.
- Jacques Vallée has argued that extraterrestrial contact could force humanity to reconsider its assumptions about morality and justice on a cosmic scale (Vallée, 1991).

3.   **Rethinking Humanity's Role**

- Alien knowledge could redefine humanity's purpose, encouraging a shift from anthropocentric thinking to a broader cosmic perspective.

6. Challenges and Risks

1.   **Technological Disparity**

- Humanity might struggle to comprehend or safely utilize alien technologies, leading to potential misuse or unintended consequences.
- Stanton Friedman warned that the rapid introduction of advanced technology could destabilize societies if not carefully managed (Friedman, 2008).

2.   **Ethical Concerns**

○   The monopolization or militarization of alien technologies could exacerbate global inequalities and conflicts.

○   Dr. Steven Greer advocates for transparency and international cooperation to ensure that such knowledge benefits all humanity (Greer, 2017).

3.   **Existential Risks**

○   Misunderstanding or misapplying alien knowledge could lead to catastrophic outcomes, particularly in fields like artificial intelligence or energy systems.

Looking Ahead

The introduction of alien knowledge would mark a new era in human history, offering transformative opportunities and significant challenges. By approaching this knowledge with curiosity, humility, and a commitment to ethical collaboration, humanity can harness its potential to build a better future for all.

Sources

1.   Alcubierre, M. (1994). "The Warp Drive: Hyper-Fast Travel Within General Relativity." *Classical and Quantum Gravity*, 11(5), L73–L77.

2.   Dyson, F. (1960). "Search for Artificial Stellar Sources of Infrared Radiation." *Science*, 131(3414), 1667–1668.

3.   Freitas, R. A. (1999). *Nanomedicine, Volume I: Basic Capabilities*. Landes Bioscience.

4.   Friedman, S. (2008). *Flying Saucers and Science: A Scientist Investigates the Mysteries of UFOs*. New Page Books.

5.   Greer, S. (2017). *Unacknowledged: An Exposé of the World's Greatest Secret*. A&M Publishing.

6.   Kaku, M. (2008). *Physics of the Impossible: A Scientific Exploration into the World of Phasers, Force Fields, Teleportation, and Time Travel*. Doubleday.

7.   Kaku, M. (2011). *The Physics of the Future: How Science Will Shape Human Destiny and Our Daily Lives by the Year 2100*. Doubleday.

8.   Mack, J. E. (1994). *Abduction: Human Encounters with Aliens*. Scribner.

9.   Vallée, J. (1991). *Dimensions: A Casebook of Alien Contact*. Ballantine Books.

Part V: Theories and Speculations

27

The Zoo Hypothesis

> *It's entirely plausible that extraterrestrial civilizations are watching humanity, studying us as anthropologists study remote tribes, while refraining from direct interaction.*
> — Dr. John A. Ball

The **Zoo Hypothesis**, first proposed by astronomer Dr. John A. Ball in 1973, suggests that advanced extraterrestrial civilizations might be deliberately avoiding contact with Earth to allow humanity to evolve naturally, much like researchers observing animals in a wildlife reserve. This theory provides a possible explanation for the Fermi Paradox—why, despite the high probability of extraterrestrial life, we have not yet detected any evidence of it. This chapter explores the Zoo Hypothesis, examining its implications, supporting arguments, and potential challenges, with insights from leading scientists and researchers.

1. Origins of the Zoo Hypothesis

1. **Dr. John A. Ball's Proposal**

   ○ In 1973, Dr. John A. Ball published a paper in *Icarus*, proposing that advanced civilizations might have ethical or scientific reasons for avoiding direct contact with humanity.

○   Ball suggested that extraterrestrials could view humanity as an emerging civilization and that their non-intervention policy reflects a form of cosmic ethics (Ball, 1973).

2.   **Relation to the Fermi Paradox**

○   The Fermi Paradox, articulated by physicist Enrico Fermi, questions why we haven't encountered extraterrestrials given the vast number of habitable planets in the galaxy.

○   The Zoo Hypothesis offers a potential resolution, positing that advanced civilizations are purposefully concealing their presence.

2. Ethical and Philosophical Underpinnings

1.   **Non-Interference Principle**

○   The Zoo Hypothesis aligns with the principle of non-interference, similar to the *Prime Directive* in *Star Trek*, which prohibits advanced civilizations from interfering with less developed ones.

○   This principle could reflect a moral code aimed at preserving the natural evolution of emerging species.

2.   **Anthropological Parallels**

- ◦ Anthropologists observing uncontacted tribes often adopt a hands-off approach to avoid disrupting their culture and way of life.
- ◦ Carl Sagan likened the idea of extraterrestrial non-interference to humanity's study of isolated ecosystems, emphasizing the importance of preserving their integrity (Sagan, 1994).

3. Scientific Arguments Supporting the Hypothesis

1. Technological Superiority

- ◦ Advanced civilizations may possess technology that allows them to observe Earth undetected, such as cloaking devices or higher-dimensional observation methods.
- ◦ Jacques Vallée proposed that UFO sightings might represent glimpses of such advanced technology, with extraterrestrials choosing when and how to reveal themselves (Vallée, 1991).

2. Biosphere as a Data Source

- ◦ Earth's diverse biosphere and human culture could provide valuable data for extraterrestrial scientists studying planetary evolution and intelligence.
- ◦ Dr. Seth Shostak of SETI has speculated that extraterrestrials might monitor Earth remotely to gather data without interfering (Shostak, 2011).

4. Counterarguments and Challenges

1. Why Not Intervene?

- ○ Critics argue that if extraterrestrials are observing Earth, they might intervene to prevent human self-destruction or environmental collapse.
- ○ Dr. Steven Greer has suggested that sightings of UFOs near nuclear facilities might represent limited interventions to safeguard planetary stability (Greer, 2017).

2. Technological Limitations

- ○ Some skeptics question whether any civilization could achieve the technological capabilities required for undetectable, long-term observation.

3. Alternative Explanations

- ○ The absence of extraterrestrial contact could be due to other factors, such as the vast distances between civilizations or the possibility that intelligent life is exceedingly rare.

5. Implications of the Zoo Hypothesis

1. **Human Self-Reflection**

   - The idea that humanity is being observed like animals in a zoo forces us to confront our own behaviors and societal flaws.
   - Carl Sagan noted that the prospect of extraterrestrial observation might encourage humanity to adopt more ethical and sustainable practices (Sagan, 1994).

2. **Cosmic Ethics**

   - If the Zoo Hypothesis is correct, it suggests that advanced civilizations adhere to a moral framework that prioritizes non-interference over exploitation or domination.
   - This could inspire humanity to consider its own ethical responsibilities when exploring space or encountering less advanced life forms.

3. **Scientific Curiosity and Preparedness**

   - The possibility of being observed underscores the importance of continuing scientific research into extraterrestrial life and developing protocols for potential contact.

6. Insights from Key Figures

1. **Dr. John A. Ball**

   - Ball emphasized the importance of considering extraterrestrial ethics and motivations, arguing that non-interference might be a deliberate choice by advanced civilizations (Ball, 1973).

2. **Carl Sagan**

   - Sagan viewed the Zoo Hypothesis as a humbling reminder of humanity's limitations and the vastness of the universe. He believed it could encourage intellectual humility and curiosity (Sagan, 1994).

3. **Jacques Vallée**

   - Vallée suggested that UFO phenomena might represent a controlled form of contact, with extraterrestrials revealing themselves selectively to study human reactions (Vallée, 1991).

4. **Dr. Steven Greer**

○ Greer proposed that extraterrestrials might adopt a policy of limited intervention, appearing only in critical moments to ensure planetary stability (Greer, 2017).

Looking Ahead

The Zoo Hypothesis invites humanity to consider the possibility that extraterrestrial civilizations are observing us from the shadows, respecting our evolutionary process while gathering data about our progress. Whether this theory reflects reality or remains speculative, it highlights the importance of ethical and scientific preparation for potential contact with advanced beings.

Sources

1. Ball, J. A. (1973). "The Zoo Hypothesis." *Icarus*, 19(3), 347–349.
2. Greer, S. (2017). *Unacknowledged: An Exposé of the World's Greatest Secret*. A&M Publishing.
3. Sagan, C. (1994). *Pale Blue Dot: A Vision of the Human Future in Space*. Random House.
4. Shostak, S. (2011). "Could They Be Watching Us?" *SETI Institute Lectures*.
5. Vallée, J. (1991). *Dimensions: A Casebook of Alien Contact*. Ballantine Books.

28

Panspermia

> The idea that life originated elsewhere and seeded
> Earth opens new perspectives on our biological roots,
> cosmic interconnectedness, and even the possibility of
> humans as carriers of extraterrestrial lineage.
> — Sir Fred Hoyle

The theory of **panspermia** proposes that life, or the building blocks of life, originated elsewhere in the universe and was transported to Earth via comets, asteroids, or interstellar dust. This concept not only reframes the question of life's origins but also intersects with metaphysical ideas such as **starseeds**, which suggest that human souls may have extraterrestrial origins. In this chapter, we examine the scientific foundations of panspermia alongside the philosophical and spiritual implications tied to the concept of starseeds.

1. What Is Panspermia?

1. **Definition and Types**

   ○ Panspermia posits that life or its precursors are distributed across the universe, capable of seeding planets with the right conditions. Variants include:

- **Lithopanspermia**: Transfer of microorganisms or organic material between planets in a solar system via meteorites.
- **Radiopanspermia**: Life traveling on interstellar dust propelled by radiation pressure.
- **Directed Panspermia**: Intentional seeding of life by advanced extraterrestrial civilizations (Crick & Orgel, 1973).

2. Historical Context

- Greek philosopher Anaxagoras was among the first to suggest that life exists throughout the cosmos.
- Modern interest began with Svante Arrhenius in the early 20th century, who proposed radiopanspermia (Arrhenius, 1908).

2. Evidence Supporting Panspermia

1. Microbial Resilience

- Experiments have shown that extremophiles, such as *Deinococcus radiodurans*, can survive space conditions, including high radiation, vacuum, and extreme temperatures (Rothschild & Mancinelli, 2001).
- Microbial survival on meteorites has been demonstrated in studies aboard the International Space Station (Horneck et al., 2008).

2.   **Organic Molecules in Space**

- ◦   Organic compounds, including amino acids and nucle-obases, have been discovered in meteorites, comets, and interstellar clouds.
- ◦   The Murchison meteorite (1969) contained over 70 amino acids, some not found naturally on Earth (Pizzarello et al., 2001).

3.   **Interplanetary Material Exchange**

- ◦   Meteorites from Mars, found on Earth, suggest material can travel between planets, potentially carrying microbial life (Weiss et al., 2000).

3. Directed Panspermia

1.   **Francis Crick's Hypothesis**

- ◦   Nobel laureate Francis Crick and Leslie Orgel proposed that advanced civilizations might have intentionally seeded life on Earth, citing the complexity of DNA as evidence of a directed origin (Crick & Orgel, 1973).

2.   **Ethical and Technological Implications**

○ Directed panspermia suggests that humans may one day assume responsibility for seeding life elsewhere, continuing the cosmic cycle.

4. The Concept of Starseeds

1. What Are Starseeds?

○ The term "starseed" refers to individuals who believe their souls or consciousness originated in extraterrestrial civilizations. This metaphysical concept aligns with panspermia in its suggestion of cosmic origins for life, albeit in a spiritual context.

2. Starseeds and Cosmic Connection

○ Proponents like Dolores Cannon and Dr. Michael Salla argue that starseeds are here to assist in humanity's evolution, carrying wisdom from advanced extraterrestrial civilizations (Cannon, 1998; Salla, 2004).

○ This belief resonates with the idea that humans might be carriers of extraterrestrial genetic or spiritual lineage, possibly seeded through directed panspermia.

3. Scientific and Philosophical Overlap

- While starseed beliefs are metaphysical, they intersect with scientific panspermia in their shared premise of life as a universal phenomenon interconnected across space.
- Sir Fred Hoyle's concept of a "cosmic ancestry" reinforces the idea that life is part of a larger, interconnected cosmic web (Hoyle & Wickramasinghe, 1981).

5. Challenges to Panspermia

1. **Survival During Transit**

   - Critics argue that exposure to space radiation and extreme conditions would destroy most organic material or microorganisms.
   - However, shielding within meteorites or ice could protect life, as experiments have shown (Nicholson et al., 2000).

2. **Ambiguity in Evidence**

   - Organic molecules in meteorites could also have formed through abiotic processes, making it difficult to prove panspermia definitively.

3. **Origins Question Unanswered**

- While panspermia explains how life may have spread, it does not address how life originated in the first place.

6. Implications of Panspermia

1. **Life as a Universal Phenomenon**

   - If panspermia is correct, it suggests that life is not unique to Earth but a common feature of the universe.
   - This aligns with the metaphysical idea that humans are part of a broader cosmic network.

2. **Cosmic Evolution**

   - Directed panspermia and starseed theories suggest a purposeful element to life's distribution, potentially guided by higher intelligence.

3. **Search for Life Beyond Earth**

   - The theory highlights the importance of exploring Mars, Europa, Enceladus, and exoplanets for signs of shared biological ancestry.

7. Insights from Key Figures

1. **Francis Crick and Leslie Orgel**

   ◦ Proposed directed panspermia as a solution to the rapid emergence of complex life on Earth, emphasizing the potential role of extraterrestrial civilizations (Crick & Orgel, 1973).

2. **Sir Fred Hoyle and Chandra Wickramasinghe**

   ◦ Advocated for cosmic panspermia, presenting evidence of microbial life in comets and suggesting that life is an inherent feature of the universe (Hoyle & Wickramasinghe, 1981).

3. **Dolores Cannon**

   ◦ Explored starseeds as a metaphysical counterpart to panspermia, linking humanity's spiritual evolution to extraterrestrial origins (Cannon, 1998).

Looking Ahead

The theory of panspermia, coupled with the concept of starseeds, invites humanity to reconsider its biological and spiritual origins. While scientific evidence continues to build, the idea also sparks philosophical and metaphysical discussions about humanity's connection to the cosmos and its role in the universe.

Sources

1. Arrhenius, S. (1908). *Worlds in the Making: The Evolution of the Universe*. Harper & Brothers.

2. Cannon, D. (1998). *The Custodians: Beyond Abduction*. Ozark Mountain Publishing.

3. Crick, F., & Orgel, L. (1973). "Directed Panspermia." *Icarus*, 19(3), 341–346.

4. Horneck, G., et al. (2008). "Microbial Survival in Space." *Advances in Space Research*, 42(6), 898–902.

5. Hoyle, F., & Wickramasinghe, C. (1981). *Evolution from Space: A Theory of Cosmic Creationism*. J.M. Dent & Sons.

6. Nicholson, W. L., et al. (2000). "Resistance of Bacillus Endospores to Extreme Terrestrial and Extraterrestrial Environments." *Microbiology and Molecular Biology Reviews*, 64(3), 548–572.

7. Pizzarello, S., et al. (2001). "The Organic Content of the Murchison Meteorite: A Modern Analysis." *Geochimica et Cosmochimica Acta*, 65(6), 1259–1273.

8. Rothschild, L. J., & Mancinelli, R. L. (2001). "Life in Extreme Environments." *Nature*, 409(6823), 1092–1101.

9. Salla, M. (2004). *Exopolitics: Political Implications of the Extraterrestrial Presence*. Exopolitics Institute.

10. Weiss, B. P., et al. (2000). "Magnetization of Martian Meteorite ALH84001 and Timing of Magnetization Events." *Science*, 290(5492), 791–795.

29

Time-Traveling Aliens

> **Could extraterrestrial visitors be future versions of humanity, traveling across time to study or influence their own past?**
> — Dr. Michael P. Masters

The theory that extraterrestrials could be time-traveling humans offers a fascinating alternative to the idea of beings from distant planets. This concept suggests that what we perceive as alien encounters might instead be instances of future humans visiting their ancestors to observe or influence pivotal moments in history. Biblical accounts, such as the story in *Daniel 10*, where a spiritual being describes a delay caused by a cosmic struggle, have been interpreted by some scholars as evidence of time travel. This chapter explores the scientific, theological, and cultural implications of this provocative theory, drawing on the work of Dr. Michael P. Masters, Jacques Vallée, and others.

1. Time Travel in Science

1. Theoretical Foundations

- Time travel is rooted in Einstein's theory of relativity, which shows that time is not an absolute constant but can be stretched or compressed by gravity or velocity.

- Kip Thorne and other physicists have proposed that traversable wormholes could act as shortcuts through spacetime, potentially enabling time travel (Thorne, 1994).

2. Advanced Civilizations and Time Manipulation

- An advanced civilization with sufficient knowledge of physics might develop technology to traverse timelines.
- Dr. Michael P. Masters, an anthropologist, argues in *Identified Flying Objects* (2019) that UFOs and their occupants might be future humans using time travel to study their origins.

2. Biblical Interpretations and Time Travel

1. The Story in *Daniel 10*

- In *Daniel 10*, a spiritual being (often interpreted as an angel) appears to the prophet Daniel after 21 days of delay. The being explains that it was detained by the "Prince of Persia" and required assistance from the archangel Michael to reach Daniel.
- Some scholars interpret this as evidence of interdimensional or timeline traversal, as the being responds to Daniel's pleas yet describes events occurring outside human perception of time.

2.   **Time and Divine Beings**

- ◦   Biblical descriptions of angels often depict them as existing outside human time constraints, reinforcing the idea that they operate in a multidimensional or nonlinear reality.
- ◦   Jacques Vallée has suggested that historical accounts of angels, gods, and otherworldly beings might be misunderstood descriptions of time-traveling entities (Vallée, 1991).

3. Evidence Supporting the Time-Traveling Alien Hypothesis

1.   **Anatomical Similarities**

- ◦   Many UFO witnesses describe extraterrestrials as humanoid, with features that could plausibly result from human evolution: large heads, small bodies, and reduced sexual dimorphism.
- ◦   Dr. Masters argues that these traits align with the evolutionary trajectory of Homo sapiens, suggesting that "aliens" might be humans from a distant future (Masters, 2019).

2.   **Temporal Paradoxes in UFO Encounters**

- ◦   Reports of UFOs often describe vehicles with characteristics that defy conventional physics, such as anti-gravity propulsion or sudden accelerations. These anomalies could indicate advanced temporal manipulation technologies.

3. **Recurrent Historical Patterns**

- ◦ UFO sightings and interactions often cluster around significant historical or technological events, such as the advent of nuclear weapons, which might suggest that time-traveling visitors are monitoring key moments in human history (Greer, 2017).

4. Challenges to the Theory

1. **Temporal Paradoxes**

- ◦ Time travel raises complex questions, such as the **grandfather paradox** (if a traveler changes the past, does their future cease to exist?).
- ◦ Some theories, like the **multiverse hypothesis**, suggest that altering the past might create alternate timelines rather than affecting the traveler's original timeline.

2. **Technological Plausibility**

- ◦ While time travel is theoretically possible, the energy requirements and technological challenges remain insurmountable with current human understanding.
- ◦ Critics argue that the time-traveling alien hypothesis relies on speculative future technologies.

3.   **Lack of Direct Evidence**

   ◦   Despite intriguing accounts, there is no direct evidence to confirm that UFOs are time machines or that their occupants are future humans.

5. Implications of Time-Traveling Aliens

1.   **Rethinking Extraterrestrial Life**

   ◦   If UFOs represent future humans rather than beings from other planets, this would redefine humanity's understanding of its place in the cosmos.
   ◦   It suggests that humanity's destiny is intertwined with its past, emphasizing the importance of historical preservation and ethical responsibility.

2.   **Ethics of Temporal Intervention**

   ◦   The idea of time-traveling humans raises questions about the ethics of interfering with the past. Are they here to observe, correct mistakes, or guide humanity toward a better future?

3.   **Philosophical and Theological Reflections**

- The concept of time-traveling aliens aligns with religious and philosophical ideas about the cyclical nature of time and the interconnectedness of past, present, and future.

6. Insights from Key Figures

1. **Dr. Michael P. Masters**

   - Masters argues that the anatomical and technological characteristics of UFO occupants suggest they are time travelers from humanity's future, studying their ancestors to better understand their origins (Masters, 2019).

2. **Jacques Vallée**

   - Vallée theorizes that UFOs and their occupants might be interdimensional beings, including possible time travelers, whose presence has been misinterpreted throughout history (Vallée, 1991).

3. **Dr. Steven Greer**

   - Greer highlights that UFO sightings often cluster around significant events, suggesting that their occupants might be monitoring pivotal moments in human history (Greer, 2017).

4.   **Biblical Scholars**

 ◦   Scholars interpreting *Daniel 10* and other biblical accounts suggest that beings described as angels or divine messengers could be operating across timelines or dimensions, offering spiritual guidance tied to humanity's cosmic evolution.

Looking Ahead

The idea of time-traveling aliens challenges humanity to expand its understanding of extraterrestrial life, time, and its own evolutionary trajectory. Whether they represent future humans or advanced interdimensional beings, their presence in historical and contemporary accounts invites us to question the boundaries of science, theology, and reality itself.

Sources

1.   Greer, S. (2017). *Unacknowledged: An Exposé of the World's Greatest Secret*. A&M Publishing.
2.   Masters, M. P. (2019). *Identified Flying Objects: A Multidisciplinary Scientific Approach to the UFO Phenomenon*. Masters Creative LLC.
3.   Thorne, K. S. (1994). *Black Holes and Time Warps: Einstein's Outrageous Legacy*. W.W. Norton & Company.
4.   Vallée, J. (1991). *Dimensions: A Casebook of Alien Contact*. Ballantine Books.
5.   The Holy Bible, New International Version (NIV). *Daniel 10*.

6. Hawking, S. (1988). *A Brief History of Time*. Bantam.

30

Multiverse and Parallel Universes

> **The universe is not only stranger than we imagine, but stranger than we can imagine. What if aliens exist not in our universe, but in alternate dimensions or parallel realities**
> — J.B.S. Haldane

The idea of a **multiverse**—a collection of universes existing alongside our own—has fascinated scientists, philosophers, and theologians alike. This concept suggests that extraterrestrials might reside in alternate dimensions or parallel universes, making them invisible or inaccessible to us under normal circumstances. The *Book of Enoch*, a non-canonical ancient Jewish text, has been interpreted by some scholars as describing interdimensional beings and realms that align with modern theories of the multiverse. This chapter explores the scientific, theological, and cultural implications of these ideas, drawing on the work of physicists, theologians, and ancient texts.

1. The Science of the Multiverse

1. What Is the Multiverse?

- ○   The multiverse hypothesis proposes that our universe is one of many, each with its own physical laws, constants, and dimensions.
- ○   There are several multiverse models, including:

  - **Bubble Universes**: Universes created by inflationary processes, each existing in its own "bubble" (Guth, 1981).
  - **Quantum Multiverse**: Based on quantum mechanics, suggesting that every decision spawns alternate realities (Everett, 1957).
  - **Brane Theory**: Postulated by string theory, where parallel universes (branes) exist in higher-dimensional space (Randall & Sundrum, 1999).

2.   **Dimensions Beyond the Observable**

- ○   String theory suggests the existence of additional spatial dimensions beyond the three we perceive. Advanced beings might inhabit or traverse these higher dimensions, appearing as "interdimensional" entities to us (Greene, 2000).

2. Parallel Universes and Extraterrestrial Life

1.   Aliens in Alternate Dimensions

- ○   If parallel universes exist, extraterrestrials might reside in these realms, operating under entirely different physical laws.

- Jacques Vallée speculated that UFO phenomena could represent beings from parallel dimensions, manifesting in our reality temporarily (Vallée, 1991).

2.   Interdimensional Travel

- Advanced civilizations might possess the technology to traverse dimensions, explaining sightings of UFOs that seem to defy conventional physics.
- The idea of "portals" or "gateways" between dimensions is supported by theoretical physics and echoed in ancient texts.

3. The Book of Enoch and Interdimensional Realms

1.   The Book of Enoch

- The *Book of Enoch*, written around the 3rd century BC, describes visions of heavens, realms, and beings not of this Earth.
- Enoch, the seventh patriarch from Adam, is taken on a journey through these realms by angelic beings, witnessing "hidden things" beyond the physical world (1 Enoch 14:8-25).

2.   Interdimensional Beings

- The Watchers, described in the *Book of Enoch*, are celestial beings who descend to Earth and interact with humans, suggesting they operate across dimensions (1 Enoch 6:1-2).
- Some scholars interpret these descriptions as ancient accounts of interdimensional entities who enter and exit our reality.

3. **The Realm of the Spirits**

- Enoch describes a "place of fire, light, and wind," a realm beyond human comprehension (1 Enoch 17:1-6). This aligns with modern ideas of alternate dimensions existing beyond our sensory perception.

4. **Modern Interpretations**

- Scholars like Dr. Michael S. Heiser suggest that the *Book of Enoch* provides a framework for understanding interdimensional phenomena, where ancient spiritual beings may parallel modern descriptions of aliens (Heiser, 2015).

4. Evidence and Theories Supporting Interdimensional Aliens

1. **UFO Phenomena and Physics**

- ○ UFO sightings often involve objects that seem to violate physical laws, such as instantaneous acceleration or appearing and disappearing without a trace.
- ○ These behaviors could be explained if the objects are transitioning between dimensions rather than traveling through space.

2. Quantum Mechanics and Consciousness

- ○ Some researchers propose that interdimensional contact might involve quantum entanglement or interactions with consciousness, as these phenomena appear to bridge dimensions.
- ○ Dr. Michio Kaku suggests that advanced beings could manipulate higher dimensions, appearing to us as "supernatural" (Kaku, 2014).

3. Portals and Anomalous Zones

- ○ Locations such as Skinwalker Ranch and the Bermuda Triangle are often cited as potential interdimensional portals due to the frequency of anomalous activity reported there (Knapp & Kelleher, 2005).

5. Challenges to the Multiverse Theory

1. Scientific Proof

- While mathematically plausible, the multiverse hypothesis remains unproven due to the lack of observable evidence.
- Critics argue that the theory, while elegant, may be unfalsifiable, placing it outside the realm of empirical science.

2. **Cognitive and Interpretive Barriers**

- Human perception and understanding are limited by three spatial dimensions, making it difficult to conceptualize or interact with higher-dimensional beings.

3. **Philosophical Implications**

- The existence of parallel universes raises questions about free will, identity, and the nature of reality itself.

6. Implications of the Multiverse and Interdimensional Aliens

1. **Redefining Reality**

- The multiverse concept challenges humanity's understanding of existence, suggesting that reality is far more complex than previously imagined.

2.   **Religious and Spiritual Paradigms**

- ◦   The alignment between the *Book of Enoch* and modern theories of alternate dimensions suggests that ancient texts may hold insights into the nature of interdimensional beings.

3.   **Future Exploration**

- ◦   Research into quantum mechanics, string theory, and anomalous phenomena may one day provide tools for exploring interdimensional realms.

7. Insights from Key Figures

1.   **Jacques Vallée**

- ◦   Vallée's work emphasizes that UFO phenomena may represent interdimensional encounters rather than extraterrestrial visitations (Vallée, 1991).

2.   **Dr. Michio Kaku**

- ◦   Kaku posits that advanced civilizations might operate in higher dimensions, using these as shortcuts for travel or observation (Kaku, 2014).

3. **Dr. Michael S. Heiser**

   ○ Heiser connects ancient accounts in the *Book of Enoch* to modern theories of interdimensional beings, suggesting that these texts may describe encounters with entities from alternate realities (Heiser, 2015).

Looking Ahead

The multiverse theory and the possibility of interdimensional aliens invite humanity to expand its understanding of existence and consider that life—and intelligence—may operate in realms beyond our perception. Exploring these ideas requires integrating science, theology, and philosophy to uncover the profound mysteries of the cosmos.

Sources

1. Everett, H. (1957). "Relative State Formulation of Quantum Mechanics." *Reviews of Modern Physics*, 29(3), 454–462.
2. Greene, B. (2000). *The Elegant Universe: Superstrings, Hidden Dimensions, and the Quest for the Ultimate Theory*. W.W. Norton & Company.
3. Guth, A. (1981). "Inflationary Universe: A Possible Solution to the Horizon and Flatness Problems." *Physical Review D*, 23(2), 347–356.
4. Heiser, M. S. (2015). *The Unseen Realm: Recovering the Supernatural Worldview of the Bible*. Lexham Press.
5. Kaku, M. (2014). *The Future of the Mind: The Scientific Quest to Understand, Enhance, and Empower the Mind*. Doubleday.

6.   Knapp, G., & Kelleher, C. (2005). *Hunt for the Skinwalker: Science Confronts the Unexplained at a Remote Ranch in Utah.* Paraview Pocket Books.

7.   Randall, L., & Sundrum, R. (1999). "Large Mass Hierarchy from a Small Extra Dimension." *Physical Review Letters*, 83(17), 3370–3373.

8.   Vallée, J. (1991). *Dimensions: A Casebook of Alien Contact.* Ballantine Books.

9.   The Holy Bible: *Book of Enoch*, Chapters 6 and 17, translations by R.H. Charles.

31

Simulation Theory and ETs

> **What if our reality is not the base level of existence but a sophisticated simulation, created and controlled by an advanced extraterrestrial civilization? Could the experience of life be an experiment or schooling designed for growth, as starseeds believe?**
> — Nick Bostrom

Simulation theory suggests that our reality could be an artificial construct created by an advanced intelligence. While originally a philosophical concept, the theory has gained traction among scientists, technologists, and spiritual thinkers. It intersects with starseed beliefs, which propose that human existence is a learning process designed by advanced extraterrestrial beings to foster growth and evolution. This chapter explores the implications of simulation theory, its connection to extraterrestrial hypotheses, and the starseed perspective that frames life as a cosmic schooling experience.

1. The Basis of Simulation Theory

1. Nick Bostrom's Simulation Argument

- Philosopher Nick Bostrom posited in 2003 that if advanced civilizations can create simulations indistinguishable from reality, it is statistically probable that we are living in a simulation (Bostrom, 2003).

- Bostrom's argument hinges on three possibilities:

  - Advanced civilizations never reach technological maturity.
  - Advanced civilizations lose interest in creating simulations.
  - We are likely living in a simulation.

2. Technological Plausibility

- Advances in computing and artificial intelligence suggest that creating hyper-realistic simulations is theoretically possible. Virtual reality and AI are seen as stepping stones toward constructing entire simulated realities.
- Dr. Silas Beane has explored how the limitations of simulations, such as computational grid structures, might leave detectable signatures in our reality (Beane et al., 2014).

3. The Role of Advanced Extraterrestrial Civilizations

- The Kardashev Scale measures civilizations by their energy usage. A Type II or III civilization could potentially harness energy from entire stars or galaxies, making simulation creation feasible (Kardashev, 1964).

- Such civilizations might run simulations to study their past, experiment with alternate outcomes, or foster spiritual or intellectual growth.

2. Starseeds and the Concept of a Cosmic Schooling

1. **What Are Starseeds?**

    - Starseeds are individuals who believe their souls originate from otherworldly or interdimensional realms. They view life on Earth as part of a cosmic learning process designed by advanced beings (Cannon, 1998).
    - Dolores Cannon, a regression therapist, described starseeds as participants in a universal schooling system, where Earth serves as a challenging but rewarding environment for spiritual evolution.

2. **Life as a Simulation for Growth**

    - Starseeds believe Earth is a "training ground" where souls experience duality, conflict, and growth to achieve higher consciousness.
    - This aligns with simulation theory in its suggestion that reality is intentionally designed to test and teach.

3. **The Role of Extraterrestrial Overseers**

- Starseed theories often depict extraterrestrial beings as mentors or guides overseeing the simulation. These beings are said to observe human progress and intervene subtly when necessary.

3. Evidence and Arguments for Simulation Theory

1.   Quantum Mechanics and Reality's Fabric

- The probabilistic nature of quantum mechanics, where particles behave unpredictably until observed, resembles computational processes in simulations (Zohar, 1990).
- Theoretical physicist James Gates discovered error-correcting codes embedded in the equations of supersymmetry, which some interpret as potential evidence of a simulated universe (Gates, 2010).

2.   The Fermi Paradox and Simulation Theory

- The absence of detectable extraterrestrial civilizations could be explained by the simulation theory, where aliens exist outside the simulated environment or control its parameters.
- Jacques Vallée speculated that UFO phenomena might represent "administered" events, reinforcing the simulation model (Vallée, 1991).

3. Psychological and Metaphysical Experiences

- Near-death experiences, déjà vu, and synchronicities are often cited as potential "glitches" or intentional features of a simulated reality designed to prompt spiritual awakening.

4. Challenges to the Theory

1. Falsifiability and Evidence

- Critics argue that simulation theory is unfalsifiable, making it more philosophical than scientific.
- Others suggest that the lack of definitive evidence limits its practical application, though this does not disprove the theory.

2. The Problem of Infinite Regression

- If we live in a simulation, who created the base reality? Does it lead to an endless chain of simulations within simulations?

3. Ethical Implications

- Simulation theory raises ethical questions: Are simulated beings deserving of rights? If extraterrestrials control the simulation, what is their moral responsibility?

5. Implications of Simulation Theory and Starseed Perspectives

1.   **Human Purpose and Meaning**

   ○   Both simulation theory and starseed beliefs emphasize the idea that life is a process of learning and growth, giving existence purpose even within a simulated framework.

2.   **The Role of Extraterrestrial Intelligence**

   ○   If advanced extraterrestrials created our reality, humanity might be part of a larger cosmic experiment or collaboration, with potential for direct interaction as we progress.

3.   **Scientific and Spiritual Integration**

   ○   Simulation theory bridges science and spirituality, suggesting that advanced intelligence—whether extraterrestrial, divine, or computational—underpins reality.

6. Insights from Key Figures

1.   **Nick Bostrom**

- ○   Bostrom's work lays the philosophical foundation for simulation theory, emphasizing its plausibility given the trajectory of technological progress (Bostrom, 2003).

2.   **Dolores Cannon**

- ○   Cannon's starseed framework adds a spiritual dimension, framing life as a schooling system created by higher beings to foster growth and understanding (Cannon, 1998).

3.   **Jacques Vallée**

- ○   Vallée's research on UFOs and interdimensional phenomena suggests that some encounters may be part of a controlled or simulated reality designed to test humanity (Vallée, 1991).

4.   **James Gates**

- ○   Gates' discovery of error-correcting codes in physical equations offers a tantalizing suggestion that reality might be computationally structured (Gates, 2010).

Looking Ahead

Simulation theory and starseed beliefs challenge humanity to reconsider its understanding of reality, purpose, and extraterrestrial intelligence. Whether our existence is a cosmic experiment, a training ground, or a simulation, these perspectives invite us to explore our potential as interconnected participants in a vast and mysterious universe.

Sources

1. Beane, S. R., et al. (2014). "Constraints on the Universe as a Numerical Simulation." *The European Physical Journal A*, 50, 148.
2. Bostrom, N. (2003). "Are You Living in a Computer Simulation?" *Philosophical Quarterly*, 53(211), 243–255.
3. Cannon, D. (1998). *The Custodians: Beyond Abduction*. Ozark Mountain Publishing.
4. Gates, S. J. (2010). "Symbols of Power: Searching for Error-Correcting Codes in Fundamental Physics." *Physics World Lecture*.
5. Kaku, M. (2014). *The Future of the Mind: The Scientific Quest to Understand, Enhance, and Empower the Mind*. Doubleday.
6. Kardashev, N. S. (1964). "Transmission of Information by Extraterrestrial Civilizations." *Soviet Astronomy*, 8, 217.
7. Vallée, J. (1991). *Dimensions: A Casebook of Alien Contact*. Ballantine Books.
8. Zohar, D. (1990). *The Quantum Self: Human Nature and Consciousness Defined by the New Physics*. William Morrow & Co.

32

The Shadow Biosphere

> If alien life already exists on Earth, it might not resemble what we recognize as life. Instead, it could occupy a 'shadow biosphere,' operating parallel to known biology, evading detection due to its unique biochemistry.
> — Dr. Carol Cleland

The idea of a **shadow biosphere** suggests that life forms fundamentally different from Earth's known biology could coexist with us, yet remain undetected due to differences in biochemistry, structure, or function. Some extend this concept further, speculating that advanced extraterrestrials might walk among us, blending into human society through advanced technology or biological adaptations. This chapter examines the scientific basis for a shadow biosphere, its potential implications, and the broader question of whether alien life forms might already be present on Earth.

1. What Is the Shadow Biosphere?

1. **Definition**

   - A shadow biosphere refers to a hypothetical realm of life forms that are biochemically distinct from all known terrestrial organisms.

- These organisms might use alternative building blocks, such as arsenic instead of phosphorus, or possess non-DNA-based genetic material (Cleland & Copley, 2006).

2.   **Scientific Context**

- Earth's known life is based on carbon, water, and DNA/RNA for genetic information. A shadow biosphere could represent an entirely separate tree of life that evolved independently.

2. Evidence and Research Supporting the Shadow Biosphere

1.   Arsenic-Based Life

- In 2010, NASA researchers discovered a strain of bacteria, *GFAJ-1*, in Mono Lake, California, that can incorporate arsenic into its DNA. While controversial, this finding suggests that life could exist with alternative chemistries (Wolfe-Simon et al., 2010).

2.   Extremophiles and Unexplored Niches

- Extremophiles thrive in conditions previously thought uninhabitable, such as deep-sea vents, acidic lakes, and radioactive environments.
- These discoveries highlight the possibility that life forms with exotic biochemistries might inhabit unexplored or overlooked ecosystems on Earth.

3. **Mysterious Microbial Communities**

- ° Studies have identified microbial communities with unusual metabolic pathways that do not conform to conventional models of life, hinting at biochemically distinct organisms (Davies et al., 2009).

3. Advanced Extraterrestrial Life Among Us

1. **Blending Into Human Society**

- ° The hypothesis that extraterrestrials might walk among us is rooted in reports of humanoid aliens and shape-shifting entities, often associated with UFO phenomena.
- ° Dr. Steven Greer has suggested that advanced extraterrestrials might possess technology to mimic human appearance or integrate into society unnoticed (Greer, 2017).

2. **Historical and Cultural Accounts**

- ° Ancient texts and folklore, such as the Sumerian *Annunaki* or the Nephilim in the *Book of Enoch*, describe beings who interacted with humanity but were not entirely human.
- ° Jacques Vallée speculates that these stories could represent early accounts of extraterrestrial visitors who adapted to Earth's environment (Vallée, 1991).

3. **Modern Anecdotal Evidence**

- ○ Reports of "Men in Black" and humanoid aliens suggest the possibility of extraterrestrials actively engaging with humanity. While anecdotal, these accounts contribute to the idea that non-terrestrial beings could be among us.

4. Challenges to Detection

1. **Scientific Bias**

- ○ The search for life on Earth and elsewhere has been biased toward organisms that share known biochemistry, potentially overlooking exotic life forms.
- ○ Dr. Carol Cleland argues that this bias has prevented scientists from considering alternative forms of life that could inhabit Earth's extreme or hidden environments (Cleland, 2007).

2. **Technological Limitations**

- ○ Current tools for detecting life, such as genomic sequencing, are designed to identify organisms based on DNA and RNA. Non-DNA-based life would evade these methods.

3. **Intentional Concealment**

- ○ If extraterrestrials are present on Earth, they might actively conceal their existence using advanced technology, making detection nearly impossible with current capabilities.

5. Implications of a Shadow Biosphere

1. **Redefining Life**

- ○ Discovering a shadow biosphere would force a redefinition of life, expanding the criteria to include alternative chemistries and structures.
- ○ This broader definition would have profound implications for the search for extraterrestrial life.

2. **Biological Coexistence**

- ○ If shadow life exists, it might interact with known life in unknown ways, influencing ecosystems or even human health.

3. **Philosophical and Ethical Considerations**

- The presence of a shadow biosphere or extraterrestrial entities on Earth raises questions about humanity's place in the cosmos and its ethical obligations toward other forms of life.

6. Insights from Key Figures

1. **Dr. Carol Cleland**

   - Cleland argues that life with alternative biochemistry might exist undetected due to the limitations of current scientific frameworks (Cleland, 2007).

2. **Dr. Steven Greer**

   - Greer emphasizes that extraterrestrials could already be present on Earth, using advanced technology to interact with humanity discreetly (Greer, 2017).

3. **Jacques Vallée**

   - Vallée suggests that UFO phenomena could represent manifestations of beings or entities operating within or alongside human reality (Vallée, 1991).

Looking Ahead

Uncovering a shadow biosphere or the presence of advanced extraterrestrials on Earth would revolutionize biology, anthropology, and our understanding of the universe. Future advances in detection technologies and open-minded exploration of unconventional possibilities will be critical in addressing these profound questions.

Sources

1. Cleland, C. E., & Copley, S. D. (2006). "The Possibility of Alternative Microbial Life on Earth." *International Journal of Astrobiology*, 5(3), 175–185.
2. Cleland, C. E. (2007). *The Quest for a Universal Theory of Life: Searching for Life as We Don't Know It*. Cambridge University Press.
3. Davies, P. C. W., et al. (2009). "Signatures of a Shadow Biosphere." *Astrobiology*, 9(3), 241–249.
4. Greer, S. (2017). *Unacknowledged: An Exposé of the World's Greatest Secret*. A&M Publishing.
5. Vallée, J. (1991). *Dimensions: A Casebook of Alien Contact*. Ballantine Books.
6. Wolfe-Simon, F., et al. (2010). "A Bacterium That Can Grow by Using Arsenic Instead of Phosphorus." *Science*, 332(6034), 1163–1166.

Part VI: The Future of Humanity

33

Preparing for Contact

> **The first contact with extraterrestrial civilizations would be a pivotal moment in human history, reshaping our understanding of ourselves and the universe. Are we ready for it—or has it already happened?**
> — Dr. Steven Greer

The prospect of first contact with extraterrestrial civilizations has been a subject of scientific, philosophical, and political preparation. From government protocols to grassroots movements, efforts are underway to anticipate and manage the profound implications of such an event. Some researchers and whistleblowers, however, argue that contact has already occurred, citing purported agreements between extraterrestrial beings and world leaders, including the alleged meeting between President Dwight D. Eisenhower and alien entities. This chapter examines the steps being taken to prepare for contact and explores the claims that it has already happened.

1. Scientific and Institutional Preparations

1.   Protocols for First Contact

- The United Nations has frameworks for addressing extraterrestrial contact, including discussions led by the

United Nations Office for Outer Space Affairs (UN-OOSA).

   ○   The SETI (Search for Extraterrestrial Intelligence) Post-Detection Task Group has developed protocols for handling signals or evidence of alien contact, emphasizing transparency, international collaboration, and scientific rigor (Tarter, 2001).

2.   **SETI and METI Initiatives**

   ○   **SETI**: Continues to scan the skies for signals from intelligent civilizations using radio telescopes and other technologies.

   ○   **METI (Messaging Extraterrestrial Intelligence)**: Focuses on sending messages to potential extraterrestrial civilizations, such as the Arecibo Message (1974) and later attempts like the Cosmic Call (1999).

   ○   Dr. Douglas Vakoch, president of METI, emphasizes the importance of crafting messages that reflect humanity's diversity and values (Vakoch, 2014).

3.   **Astrobiology Research**

   ○   Scientists are studying extreme environments on Earth and other celestial bodies to understand where and how life might arise elsewhere.

   ○   Missions to Mars, Europa, and Enceladus aim to detect microbial life, which could represent the first step toward broader extraterrestrial discovery.

2. Government Involvement and Alleged Cover-Ups

1. **The Eisenhower Meeting Allegation**

   - One of the most controversial claims about prior contact involves President Dwight D. Eisenhower allegedly meeting extraterrestrials in 1954 at Edwards Air Force Base.
   - According to whistleblowers like Philip Schneider and documents cited by Dr. Michael Salla, this meeting resulted in an agreement to exchange technology for permission to conduct limited human experimentation (Salla, 2004).

2. **Declassified UFO Programs**

   - The U.S. government has recently declassified information about UFOs, now referred to as Unidentified Aerial Phenomena (UAPs).
   - The establishment of the All-domain Anomaly Resolution Office (AARO) and reports such as the 2021 UAP report reflect increased transparency but also leave many questions unanswered.

3. **Claims of Secrecy**

   - Dr. Steven Greer argues that contact has already occurred but remains classified, with a small group of elites controlling extraterrestrial technologies and information (Greer, 2017).

3. Grassroots Movements and Civilian Efforts

1.   The Disclosure Movement

- Led by figures like Dr. Steven Greer, the Disclosure Project advocates for the release of classified information about extraterrestrial contact and advanced technologies.
- Greer's *Close Encounters of the Fifth Kind* initiative encourages individuals to initiate peaceful contact with extraterrestrial beings through meditation and intention (Greer, 2020).

2.   Public Messaging Campaigns

- Civilian-led initiatives, such as the Golden Record included on NASA's Voyager spacecraft, aim to introduce humanity to potential extraterrestrial audiences.

3.   Private Research and Advocacy

- Independent researchers like Jacques Vallée emphasize the need for open-minded scientific inquiry into UFOs and potential extraterrestrial encounters (Vallée, 1991).

4. Ethical and Philosophical Considerations

1. How Should Humanity Respond?

- Philosophers and scientists debate whether humanity should actively seek contact or avoid drawing attention to itself.
- Stephen Hawking warned that extraterrestrial contact might pose risks, likening it to the arrival of Europeans in the Americas (Hawking, 2010).

2. Ethical Protocols

- Protocols for first contact emphasize respect for extraterrestrial autonomy, transparency, and minimizing harm.

3. Cultural Impact

- The prospect of contact raises questions about how religious, political, and cultural systems would adapt to the knowledge of extraterrestrial civilizations.

5. Challenges to Preparation

1.   **Lack of Global Coordination**

   - While some international frameworks exist, the lack of cohesive global protocols for contact limits humanity's readiness.
   - Nations may compete rather than collaborate in the event of contact, risking conflict or secrecy.

2.   **Skepticism and Stigma**

   - The stigma surrounding UFOs and extraterrestrial research hampers serious scientific and governmental efforts.

3.   **Technological and Communication Barriers**

   - Even if contact is established, differences in biology, cognition, or culture could make communication extraordinarily difficult.

6. Insights from Key Figures

1.   **Dr. Steven Greer**

- Greer asserts that contact has already occurred and advocates for full transparency to unlock technologies that could benefit humanity, such as free energy (Greer, 2017).

2. **Dr. Douglas Vakoch**

- Vakoch emphasizes proactive efforts to send messages to extraterrestrial civilizations, arguing that humanity must be prepared to represent itself on a cosmic stage (Vakoch, 2014).

3. **Jacques Vallée**

- Vallée advocates for a scientific approach to UFO phenomena, suggesting that some encounters may already represent contact with interdimensional or extraterrestrial beings (Vallée, 1991).

4. **Dr. Michael Salla**

- Salla explores the idea of secret agreements between governments and extraterrestrials, particularly during the Eisenhower administration, as part of the emerging field of exopolitics (Salla, 2004).

Looking Ahead

Preparing for first contact requires a multidisciplinary approach, combining science, philosophy, and global collaboration. Whether contact is a future possibility or an event already shrouded in secrecy, humanity must act with openness, humility, and a commitment to ethical responsibility to navigate this transformative encounter.

Sources

1.   Greer, S. (2017). *Unacknowledged: An Exposé of the World's Greatest Secret*. A&M Publishing.
2.   Greer, S. (2020). *Close Encounters of the Fifth Kind: Contact Has Begun*. A&M Publishing.
3.   Salla, M. (2004). *Exopolitics: Political Implications of the Extraterrestrial Presence*. Exopolitics Institute.
4.   Tarter, J. (2001). "The Search for Extraterrestrial Intelligence (SETI)." *Annual Review of Astronomy and Astrophysics*, 39(1), 511–548.
5.   Vallée, J. (1991). *Dimensions: A Casebook of Alien Contact*. Ballantine Books.
6.   Vakoch, D. A. (2014). *Extraterrestrial Altruism: Evolution and Ethics in the Cosmos*. Springer.
7.   Hawking, S. (2010). *Into the Universe with Stephen Hawking*. Discovery Channel.

34

Alien Ethics

> The arrival of extraterrestrial beings would not only
> challenge our scientific and philosophical understanding
> but also demand a new ethical framework for interaction.
> — Carl Sagan

The question of how humanity should treat extraterrestrial beings—and how they might treat us—extends beyond science into the realms of ethics, philosophy, and law. Establishing principles for respectful, fair, and peaceful interactions is crucial to ensuring mutual understanding and avoiding conflict. This chapter explores the emerging field of **alien ethics**, incorporating insights from thinkers like Carl Sagan, Jacques Vallée, and Stephen Hawking.

1. Ethical Considerations for Humanity

1. **The Principle of Universal Respect**

   - Humanity must approach extraterrestrial beings with humility and respect, recognizing them as intelligent, autonomous entities.
   - Carl Sagan advocated for an ethical approach based on the "cosmic perspective," emphasizing shared existence in the universe (Sagan, 1994).

2.   **Avoiding Anthropocentrism**

- ○   Interactions with extraterrestrials should avoid imposing human-centric values or assumptions about morality and intelligence.
- ○   Jacques Vallée warns that interpreting alien behavior through a purely human lens could lead to misunderstanding or conflict (Vallée, 1991).

3.   **Non-Interference**

- ○   Drawing from the *Prime Directive* in *Star Trek*, many ethicists argue that humanity should not interfere in the development of extraterrestrial civilizations unless explicitly invited.

4.   **Resource Sharing**

- ○   Ethical frameworks should address the use of shared resources, such as planetary ecosystems or interstellar materials, ensuring mutual benefit and sustainability.

2. Ethical Challenges for Extraterrestrials

1.   **Respect for Human Autonomy**

    ○   Advanced extraterrestrial civilizations must respect humanity's sovereignty and cultural diversity, refraining from coercive or manipulative behavior.

    ○   Dr. Steven Greer suggests that some extraterrestrial encounters, such as abductions, may involve breaches of ethical norms and require accountability (Greer, 2017).

2.   Non-Exploitation

    ○   Ethical extraterrestrials should avoid exploiting Earth's resources or biological systems for their own gain.

3.   Moral Responsibility of Advanced Civilizations

    ○   As a potentially more advanced species, extraterrestrials might bear ethical responsibility for guiding or mentoring humanity without imposing their values.

    ○   Carl Sagan likened this responsibility to humanity's ethical obligations toward less technologically developed species on Earth (Sagan, 1994).

3. Frameworks for Alien Ethics

1.   International Agreements

    ○   The Outer Space Treaty (1967) prohibits the militarization of space and emphasizes peaceful exploration but lacks specific provisions for interactions with extraterrestrials (UNOOSA, 1967).

- A new global framework could address ethical guidelines for contact, resource sharing, and cultural exchange.

2.   **Relational Ethics**

- Philosopher Emmanuel Levinas' concept of ethics as a response to "the Other" could inform how humanity approaches interactions with beings fundamentally different from us (Levinas, 1969).

3.   **The Universal Declaration of Rights for Sentient Beings**

- Proposals for universal rights for sentient beings could extend ethical principles, such as the right to autonomy, non-harm, and fair treatment, to extraterrestrials (Shostak, 2011).

4. Potential Ethical Dilemmas

1.   **Conflicting Interests**

- Disputes over resources, territory, or technology could challenge ethical principles, requiring frameworks for conflict resolution.

2. **Cross-Cultural Misunderstandings**

  ◦ Differences in communication, values, or biology might lead to ethical dilemmas, as actions perceived as benign by one civilization could be harmful to another.

3. **Bioethical Considerations**

  ◦ Sharing or exchanging biological materials, such as DNA or microbes, raises concerns about contamination, exploitation, and unintended consequences.

5. Insights from Key Figures

1. **Carl Sagan**

  ◦ Sagan emphasized the importance of humility, openness, and respect in interactions with extraterrestrial civilizations, warning against anthropocentrism and assumptions of superiority (Sagan, 1994).

2. **Jacques Vallée**

  ◦ Vallée advocated for a scientific and ethical approach to UFO phenomena, highlighting the need for mutual understanding between humans and potential extraterrestrial beings (Vallée, 1991).

3.   **Stephen Hawking**

   ◦   Hawking cautioned that contact with extraterrestrials might pose risks, comparing it to historical encounters between technologically unequal human civilizations (Hawking, 2010).

4.   **Dr. Steven Greer**

   ◦   Greer promotes peaceful, ethical contact with extraterrestrials, arguing that humanity must overcome secrecy and fear to establish trust (Greer, 2017).

6. Ethical Principles for First Contact

1.   **Transparency**

   ◦   Governments and institutions should prioritize openness and public engagement to ensure ethical accountability in interactions with extraterrestrials.

2.   **Mutual Benefit**

- ° Any exchange of technology, knowledge, or resources should prioritize equitable outcomes for both humanity and extraterrestrial civilizations.

3. **Non-Violence**

- ° Peaceful approaches to contact should be the default, avoiding militarization or aggression unless in self-defense.

4. **Environmental Responsibility**

- ° Ethical frameworks should address the potential environmental impact of extraterrestrial interactions, ensuring the preservation of Earth's ecosystems.

Looking Ahead

The development of alien ethics represents a critical step in preparing for the transformative possibility of extraterrestrial contact. By fostering mutual respect, transparency, and cooperation, humanity can navigate the challenges and opportunities of contact while safeguarding its values and planetary integrity.

Sources

1. Greer, S. (2017). *Unacknowledged: An Exposé of the World's Greatest Secret.* A&M Publishing.

2.   Hawking, S. (2010). *Into the Universe with Stephen Hawking.* Discovery Channel.

3.   Levinas, E. (1969). *Totality and Infinity: An Essay on Exteriority.* Duquesne University Press.

4.   Sagan, C. (1994). *Pale Blue Dot: A Vision of the Human Future in Space.* Random House.

5.   Shostak, S. (2011). "What Happens If We Find ET?" *SETI Institute Lectures.*

6.   UNOOSA (1967). *The Outer Space Treaty.* United Nations Office for Outer Space Affairs.

7.   Vallée, J. (1991). *Dimensions: A Casebook of Alien Contact.* Ballantine Books.

35

Space Colonization

> **The discovery of extraterrestrial life could inspire humanity to expand into the cosmos, propelling us toward interstellar exploration and colonization—or has this journey already begun in secrecy?**
> — Dr. Michael Salla

The possibility of space colonization is closely tied to humanity's quest for exploration and survival. The discovery of extraterrestrial life would provide profound motivation for venturing beyond Earth, fostering technological advancements, and raising questions about humanity's role in the universe. Some researchers and whistleblowers suggest that humanity has already begun this journey through secret space programs, such as the alleged **Solar Warden**, which purports to have established bases on the Moon, Mars, and beyond. This chapter explores the implications of space colonization driven by the discovery of extraterrestrial life and examines claims about covert space operations.

1. The Motivations for Space Colonization

1. Ensuring Humanity's Survival

- Physicist Stephen Hawking argued that humanity must become a multi-planetary species to ensure survival in the face of existential threats, such as asteroid impacts, pandemics, or nuclear war (Hawking, 2008).

2. **Expanding Human Potential**

- Space colonization offers opportunities for technological, scientific, and cultural advancement, inspiring humanity to reach new frontiers.
- The discovery of extraterrestrial life would provide further motivation, as it would demonstrate that life can exist elsewhere and prompt exploration of alien ecosystems and civilizations.

3. **Interstellar Collaboration**

- Contact with extraterrestrial civilizations might lead to collaborations in space exploration, sharing technologies, and co-developing colonization strategies.

2. Technological Advances Driving Colonization

1. **Propulsion Systems**

- Breakthroughs in propulsion technology, such as ion drives, nuclear fusion, and theoretical warp drives, could enable faster travel to other planets and star systems (Alcubierre, 1994).

2. **Terraforming**

- ° Terraforming technologies could make hostile environments, such as Mars or Europa, habitable for human colonists.
- ° NASA and private companies like SpaceX are researching ways to create sustainable habitats on Mars, including generating oxygen and cultivating crops.

3. **Extraterrestrial Mining**

- ° The discovery of extraterrestrial civilizations might lead to partnerships or competition for resources on asteroids, moons, and other planets.
- ° Companies like Planetary Resources, purchased by ConsenSys Inc. in October 2018, are already exploring the potential of asteroid mining.

3. Claims of Secret Space Programs

1. **The Solar Warden Allegations**

- ° Whistleblower Gary McKinnon, who hacked into NASA and U.S. military databases, claimed to have found evidence of a secret space program called **Solar Warden** involving advanced spacecraft and bases on the Moon and Mars (Salla, 2004).

○   McKinnon described seeing references to "non-terrestrial officers" and spacecraft not listed in public records, sparking widespread speculation.

2.   **Dr. Michael Salla's Research**

○   Salla, a leading figure in exopolitics, argues that Solar Warden is part of a covert effort involving reverse-engineered extraterrestrial technology to establish human presence beyond Earth.

○   According to Salla, Solar Warden operates under international cooperation, suggesting that space colonization may already be underway (Salla, 2015).

3.   **The Role of Advanced Technologies**

○   Alleged technologies used in secret space programs include anti-gravity propulsion, zero-point energy, and cloaking devices—technologies purportedly acquired through extraterrestrial contact or reverse engineering.

4. Ethical and Political Implications of Space Colonization

1.   **Territorial Claims and Governance**

○   The Outer Space Treaty (1967) prohibits nations from claiming sovereignty over celestial bodies. However, colonization efforts raise questions about governance and resource sharing (UNOOSA, 1967).

2.   **Potential Conflicts with Extraterrestrial Life**

- ◦   Expanding into space could lead to ethical dilemmas if colonization efforts interfere with alien ecosystems or civilizations.

3.   **Equity and Inclusion**

- ◦   Critics argue that space colonization efforts could exacerbate existing inequalities, with access to space and its resources controlled by wealthy nations and corporations.

5. Inspiring Humanity Through Discovery

1.   **A New Era of Exploration**

- ◦   The discovery of extraterrestrial life could reignite humanity's passion for exploration, fostering a collective vision of expanding beyond Earth.
- ◦   Projects like the Breakthrough Starshot Initiative aim to send probes to nearby star systems, inspired by the possibility of finding life (Worden et al., 2016).

2.   **Uniting Humanity**

○   Space colonization offers an opportunity for global collaboration, transcending national and cultural boundaries to work toward a shared future among the stars.

6. Insights from Key Figures

1.   **Gary McKinnon**

○   McKinnon's claims about Solar Warden have fueled widespread speculation about secret space programs and the possibility of covert extraterrestrial collaboration.

2.   **Dr. Michael Salla**

○   Salla argues that the secret space program is evidence of advanced colonization efforts already in progress, emphasizing the need for transparency and public engagement (Salla, 2015).

3.   **Stephen Hawking**

○   Hawking emphasized the necessity of space colonization for humanity's long-term survival, advocating for investments in technology and exploration (Hawking, 2008).

4.   **Elon Musk**

- ◦   Musk's SpaceX aims to establish a human presence on Mars, driven by the belief that space colonization is essential for the survival and evolution of humanity.

Looking Ahead

The discovery of extraterrestrial life and the alleged existence of secret space programs highlight humanity's drive to explore and colonize the cosmos. Whether through public or covert efforts, space colonization represents a transformative step in human history, offering both opportunities and challenges as we navigate our place in the universe.

Sources

1.   Alcubierre, M. (1994). "The Warp Drive: Hyper-Fast Travel Within General Relativity." *Classical and Quantum Gravity*, 11(5), L73–L77.
2.   Hawking, S. (2008). "Why We Must Flee Earth." *Big Think Lecture*.
3.   Salla, M. (2004). *Exopolitics: Political Implications of the Extraterrestrial Presence*. Exopolitics Institute.
4.   Salla, M. (2015). *Insiders Reveal Secret Space Programs & Extraterrestrial Alliances*. Exopolitics Institute.
5.   UNOOSA (1967). *The Outer Space Treaty*. United Nations Office for Outer Space Affairs.
6.   Worden, P., et al. (2016). "Breakthrough Starshot: A New Vision for Interstellar Exploration." *Publications of the Astronomical Society of the Pacific*, 128(959).

36

Building Alliances

> The concept of interstellar diplomacy challenges us to consider how humanity might interact with extraterrestrial civilizations on equal footing. Could there already exist a Galactic Federation, governing relations among advanced species?
> — Dr. Haim Eshed

The idea of building alliances with extraterrestrial civilizations raises questions about humanity's role in the cosmos, the ethics of interstellar diplomacy, and the potential existence of an established **Galactic Federation Council**. This chapter explores how interstellar alliances might be imagined, structured, and navigated, while addressing claims by whistleblowers and researchers that such alliances may already exist.

1. The Foundations of Interstellar Diplomacy

1. The Need for Universal Principles

- Interstellar diplomacy requires principles that transcend human-specific norms, such as mutual respect, non-interference, and the peaceful resolution of conflicts.
- Carl Sagan emphasized the importance of adopting a "cosmic perspective," treating extraterrestrial civilizations as peers rather than subordinates (Sagan, 1994).

2.   **Learning from Earth's History**

- Diplomatic practices on Earth, such as the United Nations' model of multilateral negotiation, provide a starting point for imagining interstellar governance.
- However, past colonial encounters also serve as cautionary tales, underscoring the need for ethical approaches to interaction.

3.   **SETI and Messaging Initiatives**

- Programs like METI (Messaging Extraterrestrial Intelligence) aim to proactively communicate with extraterrestrial civilizations, fostering a foundation for future alliances (Vakoch, 2014).

2. The Galactic Federation Hypothesis

1.   **Claims by Dr. Haim Eshed**

- In 2020, Dr. Haim Eshed, former head of Israel's Defense Ministry's space directorate, claimed that a **Galactic Federation** exists and is observing humanity.
- According to Eshed, this Federation has chosen not to reveal itself until humanity demonstrates readiness, particularly in achieving global unity and stability (Eshed, 2020).

2.   **Historical Context and Whistleblower Testimonies**

- ◦   Whistleblowers allege that secret space programs have already engaged with a Galactic Federation, involving agreements on technology exchange and resource management (Salla, 2015).
- ◦   These claims often include references to advanced extraterrestrial civilizations working collaboratively to oversee and guide emerging species.

3.   **Ancient Texts and the Federation Concept**

- ◦   Interpretations of ancient texts, such as the Sumerian *Enuma Elish* and the *Book of Enoch*, suggest that extraterrestrial entities may have interacted with humanity as part of a larger cosmic order.
- ◦   These interactions, described as alliances or mentorships, resonate with modern notions of a Galactic Federation.

3. Challenges in Building Interstellar Alliances

1.   **Cultural and Biological Differences**

- ◦   Differences in cognition, communication methods, and values could complicate diplomacy, requiring the development of universal languages or symbolic systems.

2.   **Technological Imbalances**

- ° Advanced civilizations might hold significant techno-logical advantages, raising ethical concerns about exploitation or coercion.
- ° Jacques Vallée warned that unequal power dynamics could hinder genuine cooperation (Vallée, 1991).

3.   **Trust and Transparency**

- ° Establishing trust with extraterrestrial civilizations would require transparency in human governance and adherence to agreed-upon principles.

4. Imagining the Structure of a Galactic Federation

1.   **Membership and Representation**

- ° A Galactic Federation might include representatives from various civilizations, each contributing to decision-making on matters of shared interest, such as trade, exploration, and conflict resolution.

2.   **Jurisdiction and Governance**

- ○ The Federation could govern interstellar territories, regulate the use of resources, and oversee interactions between member civilizations.
- ○ Protocols might prohibit interference with less advanced species, akin to the *Prime Directive* in *Star Trek*.

3. Conflict Resolution Mechanisms

- ○ Diplomatic protocols and mediation processes would be essential for resolving disputes, ensuring peaceful coexistence among diverse civilizations.

5. Humanity's Role in Interstellar Alliances

1. Readiness for Participation

- ○ Humanity must achieve certain milestones, such as global peace, environmental sustainability, and equitable governance, to be considered a credible member of a Galactic Federation.
- ○ Dr. Eshed's claims highlight the need for unity and ethical maturity before open contact can occur.

2. Technological Contributions

- ◦ Contributions to a Galactic Federation might include advancements in artificial intelligence, quantum computing, or sustainable energy systems.

3. **Ethical Leadership**

- ◦ As a species that has grappled with its own ethical dilemmas, humanity could offer unique insights into fostering cooperation among diverse civilizations.

6. Insights from Key Figures

1. **Dr. Haim Eshed**

- ◦ Eshed's revelations suggest that humanity is under observation by a Galactic Federation, which prioritizes gradual, ethical engagement with Earth (Eshed, 2020).

2. **Carl Sagan**

- ◦ Sagan advocated for humility and openness in interstellar diplomacy, emphasizing that humanity's future depends on its ability to coexist peacefully with other intelligent beings (Sagan, 1994).

3. **Dr. Michael Salla**

   ○ Salla explores the concept of exopolitics, arguing that secret space programs have already established diplomatic relations with extraterrestrial entities, including Federation-like councils (Salla, 2015).

4. **Jacques Vallée**

   ○ Vallée highlights the importance of scientific inquiry and ethical responsibility in interactions with extraterrestrials, emphasizing the potential for mutual learning (Vallée, 1991).

Looking Ahead

Building interstellar alliances requires humanity to overcome its divisions, embrace ethical governance, and prepare for the profound responsibilities of cosmic citizenship. Whether or not a Galactic Federation already exists, the principles of diplomacy, respect, and collaboration will be essential in navigating humanity's role in the universe.

Sources

1. Eshed, H. (2020). Interview with *Yediot Aharonot*, as reported in *The Jerusalem Post*.
2. Sagan, C. (1994). *Pale Blue Dot: A Vision of the Human Future in Space*. Random House.
3. Salla, M. (2015). *Insiders Reveal Secret Space Programs & Extraterrestrial Alliances*. Exopolitics Institute.

4.   UNOOSA (1967). *The Outer Space Treaty*. United Nations Office for Outer Space Affairs.

5.   Vallée, J. (1991). *Dimensions: A Casebook of Alien Contact*. Ballantine Books.

6.   Vakoch, D. A. (2014). *Extraterrestrial Altruism: Evolution and Ethics in the Cosmos*. Springer.

37

Alien Threats

> **While extraterrestrial contact could herald profound opportunities for humanity, preparing for worst-case scenarios is essential, as we cannot assume alien intentions to be universally benevolent.**
> — Stephen Hawking

The discovery of extraterrestrial life—or direct contact with advanced civilizations—poses existential questions about how humanity might respond to alien threats. While much speculation centers on peaceful cooperation, prudence requires considering scenarios where extraterrestrials might pose risks to humanity's survival, sovereignty, or freedom. This chapter explores potential alien threats, frameworks for preparation, and historical lessons that underscore the importance of readiness for worst-case scenarios.

1. Understanding Potential Alien Threats

1. **Hostile Intentions**

    ○ Extraterrestrials might view humanity as a threat, a resource, or an obstacle to their objectives.

    ○ Stephen Hawking cautioned that alien contact could parallel historical encounters between technologically advanced and less advanced civilizations, which often led to exploitation or destruction (Hawking, 2010).

2. **Resource Competition**

- Extraterrestrials might seek Earth's resources—water, minerals, or biological materials—without regard for human welfare.
- Michio Kaku posited that resource acquisition could drive alien colonization efforts, especially if their own planetary systems face depletion (Kaku, 2018).

3. **Unintended Harm**

- Even without malicious intent, alien technologies, biological agents, or ecological disruptions could pose existential risks to humanity.
- The introduction of extraterrestrial microbes or energy systems could have catastrophic consequences for Earth's environment.

2. Historical Parallels and Lessons

1. **Colonial Encounters on Earth**

- ○ The colonization of the Americas demonstrates how technological disparity can lead to exploitation, disease outbreaks, and cultural erasure.
- ○ These historical examples serve as cautionary tales for how humanity might fare in an encounter with a more advanced civilization.

2. **Nuclear Age and Mutually Assured Destruction**

- ○ The Cold War era highlights the risks of technological escalation and the importance of diplomatic safeguards to prevent catastrophic outcomes.
- ○ These lessons could inform strategies for negotiating with potentially hostile extraterrestrials.

3. **UFO Sightings Near Military Installations**

- ○ Reports of unidentified aerial phenomena (UAPs) near nuclear facilities raise concerns about extraterrestrial surveillance of humanity's most destructive technologies.
- ○ Dr. Steven Greer has argued that such incidents could indicate extraterrestrials monitoring human weaponry to prevent accidental or intentional use (Greer, 2017).

3. Frameworks for Defense and Preparedness

1. **Planetary Defense Systems**

- ○ Existing planetary defense initiatives, such as those designed to address asteroid threats, could be adapted to include extraterrestrial scenarios.
- ○ The Space Force, established by the United States, has expanded its focus to include space-based threats, though its capabilities remain largely speculative.

2. International Collaboration

- ○ A unified global response is essential for addressing extraterrestrial threats.
- ○ The Outer Space Treaty (1967) emphasizes peaceful exploration but lacks provisions for coordinated defense against hostile alien civilizations (UNOOSA, 1967).

3. Technological Readiness

- ○ Investments in advanced weaponry, cyberdefense, and artificial intelligence could bolster humanity's ability to respond to alien threats.
- ○ Theoretical models, such as those proposed by physicist Michio Kaku, suggest that humanity must achieve Type I civilization status (global unity and energy mastery) to effectively counter extraterrestrial risks (Kaku, 2018).

4. Ethical Dilemmas in Defensive Strategies

1.   Preemptive Action vs. Diplomacy

- ◦   Should humanity attempt preemptive measures if extraterrestrial intentions appear hostile, or prioritize diplomacy to avoid escalation?
- ◦   Carl Sagan argued that diplomacy must remain the primary focus, with defense as a contingency plan (Sagan, 1994).

2.   Balancing Secrecy and Transparency

- ◦   Governments face ethical questions about how much to disclose to the public regarding alien threats and defensive measures.
- ◦   Secrecy might prevent panic but could erode trust and limit global cooperation.

3.   Collateral Damage

- ◦   Defensive actions could inadvertently harm Earth's ecosystems or non-combatant extraterrestrial entities, raising ethical concerns about proportionality and unintended consequences.

5. Potential Defensive Scenarios

1. **Alien Invasion**

    ◦ Invasion scenarios, as depicted in science fiction, might involve direct military confrontation, resource extraction, or territorial occupation.
    ◦ Effective responses would require rapid coordination between nations, leveraging all available resources and technologies.

2. **Biological or Ecological Threats**

    ◦ Alien pathogens could devastate human populations, necessitating global health responses and containment strategies.
    ◦ Extraterrestrial technologies or energy sources might destabilize Earth's ecosystems, requiring immediate mitigation efforts.

3. **Technological Disruption**

    ◦ Advanced extraterrestrial civilizations might disable human technologies, including communications, energy grids, and defense systems, to weaken humanity's ability to resist.
    ◦ Cybersecurity and decentralized infrastructure would be critical in such scenarios.

6. Insights from Key Figures

1. **Stephen Hawking**

   ◦ Hawking emphasized the importance of caution in seeking extraterrestrial contact, warning that humanity's technological and ethical immaturity might make it vulnerable to exploitation (Hawking, 2010).

2. **Dr. Michio Kaku**

   ◦ Kaku argued that humanity's best defense against extraterrestrial threats lies in advancing its own technological capabilities and achieving global unity (Kaku, 2018).

3. **Dr. Steven Greer**

   ◦ Greer advocates for peaceful engagement with extraterrestrials but acknowledges the need for preparedness in case of hostile encounters (Greer, 2017).

4. **Carl Sagan**

   ◦ Sagan believed that interstellar diplomacy and mutual respect should guide humanity's approach, but recognized the need for contingency planning in the face of uncertainty (Sagan, 1994).

Looking Ahead

While the discovery of extraterrestrial life holds immense promise, preparing for worst-case scenarios is a critical aspect of humanity's engagement with the cosmos. By investing in technology, fostering global cooperation, and developing ethical frameworks for defense, humanity can ensure it is ready to face any challenge—whether alien or terrestrial.

Sources

1. Greer, S. (2017). *Unacknowledged: An Exposé of the World's Greatest Secret*. A&M Publishing.
2. Hawking, S. (2010). *Into the Universe with Stephen Hawking*. Discovery Channel.
3. Kaku, M. (2018). *The Future of Humanity: Terraforming Mars, Interstellar Travel, Immortality, and Our Destiny Beyond Earth*. Doubleday.
4. Sagan, C. (1994). *Pale Blue Dot: A Vision of the Human Future in Space*. Random House.
5. UNOOSA (1967). *The Outer Space Treaty*. United Nations Office for Outer Space Affairs.
6. Vallée, J. (1991). *Dimensions: A Casebook of Alien Contact*. Ballantine Books.

38

The End of Isolation

> The moment humanity establishes contact with an extraterrestrial civilization, our species will enter an entirely new era, forever altering our understanding of the universe and our place within it.
> — Carl Sagan

The confirmation of extraterrestrial life would mark the end of humanity's cosmic isolation, ushering in an era of profound transformation. From scientific breakthroughs to philosophical revolutions, such an event would redefine human history. This chapter explores how alien contact could reshape humanity's trajectory, addressing the implications for science, society, culture, and our collective identity.

1. The Dawn of a New Era

1.   The Cosmic Perspective

- Contact with extraterrestrial intelligence would force humanity to adopt a broader perspective, shifting from an Earth-centric worldview to a universal one.
- Carl Sagan described this shift as essential to humanity's growth, likening it to the realization that Earth orbits the Sun—a humbling and transformative moment (Sagan, 1994).

2. **Unity in Diversity**

- ◦ The knowledge that we are not alone could foster global unity, transcending national and cultural divisions to focus on humanity's shared place in the cosmos.
- ◦ The late physicist Stephen Hawking suggested that awareness of extraterrestrial life might encourage humanity to overcome its differences in pursuit of common goals (Hawking, 2010).

2. Scientific Breakthroughs

1. **New Paradigms in Physics and Biology**

- ◦ Alien contact could introduce revolutionary technologies and scientific principles, including insights into advanced propulsion, renewable energy, and alternative biochemistries.
- ◦ Michio Kaku speculates that extraterrestrials might have solved challenges humanity still grapples with, such as quantum computing and faster-than-light travel (Kaku, 2018).

2. **Expansion of Astrobiology**

- ◦ Discovering extraterrestrial life forms would broaden the scope of astrobiology, providing new data on the conditions necessary for life and the diversity of life forms in the universe.

3.   **Technological Leapfrogging**

- ○   Reverse-engineering alien technologies could accelerate humanity's progress by centuries, transforming industries from healthcare to space exploration.

3. Cultural and Philosophical Transformations

1.   **Reexamining Humanity's Place**

- ○   The knowledge of extraterrestrial civilizations would challenge long-held beliefs about humanity's uniqueness and centrality in the universe.
- ○   Philosophers and theologians would grapple with questions about the meaning of life, the nature of consciousness, and the existence of a higher power.

2.   **Influence on Art and Culture**

- ○   Alien contact would inspire new artistic and cultural movements, reflecting humanity's evolving understanding of itself and its relationship to the cosmos.
- ○   Historical parallels, such as the space race's influence on mid-20th-century art and media, suggest that extraterres-

trial contact would leave an indelible mark on human creativity.

3. **Religious Interpretations**

- ° Religions might reinterpret doctrines to accommodate the existence of extraterrestrial life, as many already contain narratives of otherworldly beings or creation myths that could align with alien contact.

4. Ethical and Societal Challenges

1. **Global Governance and Diplomacy**

- ° Alien contact would necessitate new frameworks for global cooperation, potentially involving the establishment of interstellar diplomatic protocols.
- ° The United Nations and organizations like SETI have proposed preliminary guidelines, but comprehensive policies remain underdeveloped (Tarter, 2001).

2. **Social Adaptation**

- ° The psychological impact of alien contact could range from existential anxiety to collective euphoria. Managing public reactions would require careful communication and transparent governance.

○   Carl Jung theorized that UFO phenomena tap into humanity's archetypal fears and aspirations, suggesting that contact could catalyze both individual and societal transformation (Jung, 1959).

3.   **Ethical Interactions**

○   Establishing equitable relationships with extraterrestrial civilizations would require ethical principles, such as respect for autonomy, non-violence, and mutual benefit.

○   The challenges of understanding alien intentions and navigating potential power imbalances would demand diplomatic skill and ethical clarity.

5. Lessons from History

1.   **Colonial Encounters**

○   Historical interactions between technologically advanced and less advanced societies often resulted in exploitation and conflict.

○   These lessons underscore the need for humility and caution in approaching extraterrestrial civilizations, ensuring that humanity avoids repeating the mistakes of its past.

2.   **Scientific Revelations**

- ○ Major scientific discoveries, such as the Copernican revolution or the discovery of DNA, have fundamentally altered humanity's understanding of itself.
- ○ Alien contact would represent a similar turning point, reshaping humanity's perception of its origins, purpose, and destiny.

6. Preparing for Contact

1. **Developing Protocols**

   - ○ Organizations like SETI and METI have drafted post-detection protocols, emphasizing international collaboration, transparency, and ethical considerations (Vakoch, 2014).

2. **Fostering Resilience**

   - ○ Public education and open dialogue about the possibility of extraterrestrial life can help prepare humanity for the psychological and societal impacts of contact.

3. **Encouraging Global Unity**

   - ○ Addressing global challenges, such as climate change and inequality, would demonstrate humanity's readiness to engage as a united species.

7. Insights from Key Figures

1. **Carl Sagan**

    ○   Sagan emphasized the importance of adopting a cosmic perspective, viewing extraterrestrial contact as an opportunity for growth and self-reflection (Sagan, 1994).

2. **Stephen Hawking**

    ○   Hawking warned of potential risks but also acknowledged the transformative potential of discovering intelligent life (Hawking, 2010).

3. **Michio Kaku**

    ○   Kaku speculated that extraterrestrial contact would accelerate technological progress and challenge humanity to achieve Type I civilization status on the Kardashev scale (Kaku, 2018).

4. **Dr. Douglas Vakoch**

    ○   Vakoch advocates for proactive communication efforts and ethical engagement with extraterrestrial civilizations, emphasizing humanity's role as a responsible cosmic participant (Vakoch, 2014).

Looking Ahead

The end of humanity's cosmic isolation would mark the beginning of a transformative chapter in our history. By embracing the opportunities and challenges of extraterrestrial contact with humility, curiosity, and unity, humanity can chart a path toward a future enriched by its connection to the broader universe.

Sources

1. Hawking, S. (2010). *Into the Universe with Stephen Hawking*. Discovery Channel.

2. Jung, C. G. (1959). *Flying Saucers: A Modern Myth of Things Seen in the Skies*. Harcourt Brace.

3. Kaku, M. (2018). *The Future of Humanity: Terraforming Mars, Interstellar Travel, Immortality, and Our Destiny Beyond Earth*. Doubleday.

4. Sagan, C. (1994). *Pale Blue Dot: A Vision of the Human Future in Space*. Random House.

5. Tarter, J. (2001). "The Search for Extraterrestrial Intelligence (SETI)." *Annual Review of Astronomy and Astrophysics*, 39(1), 511–548.

6. Vakoch, D. A. (2014). *Extraterrestrial Altruism: Evolution and Ethics in the Cosmos*. Springer.

39

A New Golden Age?

> **The discovery of extraterrestrial life and their advanced technologies could usher humanity into an era of unprecedented progress—an intergalactic future marked by free energy, medical breakthroughs, and interplanetary travel.**
> — Michio Kaku

The integration of extraterrestrial knowledge and technology into human society has the potential to transform every facet of life, sparking what many imagine as a new **Golden Age**. From addressing energy and healthcare challenges to enabling interplanetary exploration, such advancements could redefine humanity's future. This chapter explores how alien technologies might propel us into an intergalactic era and examines the ethical, societal, and scientific implications of this transformation.

1. The Promise of Free Energy

1. **Zero-Point Energy**

   - Extraterrestrial civilizations are often hypothesized to harness zero-point energy, tapping into quantum fluctuations of the vacuum for limitless and sustainable power.

- ○ Dr. Steven Greer asserts that suppressed extraterrestrial technologies, including energy systems, could eliminate humanity's dependence on fossil fuels (Greer, 2017).

2. **Dyson Spheres and Energy Harvesting**

- ○ Advanced civilizations may construct megastructures, such as Dyson Spheres, to capture the total energy output of their stars, a feat humanity could emulate with their guidance (Dyson, 1960).
- ○ Adoption of such technologies could address global energy inequality and mitigate environmental degradation.

3. **Impact on Global Systems**

- ○ Free energy could revolutionize economies, eliminating energy scarcity and reducing geopolitical tensions over resource control.

2. Medical Breakthroughs and Longevity

1. **Advanced Healing Technologies**

- ○ Alien civilizations may possess regenerative medical technologies capable of curing diseases, repairing cellular damage, and even reversing aging.

- ○ Techniques like molecular nanotechnology and energy-based healing could redefine healthcare systems (Freitas, 1999).

2. **Insights into Alien Biology**

- ○ Studying extraterrestrial life forms could reveal new biological pathways, inspiring treatments for previously incurable conditions.
- ○ Michio Kaku speculates that alien understanding of DNA and consciousness could lead to breakthroughs in mental health and cognitive enhancement (Kaku, 2018).

3. **Ethical Challenges**

- ○ Access to alien medical technologies raises questions about distribution equity and the potential for misuse, such as genetic manipulation or biological warfare.

3. Interplanetary and Interstellar Travel

1. **Propulsion Advancements**

- ○ Technologies like warp drives, wormholes, or anti-gravity propulsion, theorized in physics but unattainable with current human technology, might become reality through extraterrestrial collaboration (Alcubierre, 1994).

2.   **Colonization of the Solar System**

- ◦   With alien assistance, humanity could establish self-sustaining colonies on Mars, Europa, and beyond, overcoming barriers like radiation, life support, and resource scarcity.
- ◦   SpaceX founder Elon Musk envisions a multiplanetary future for humanity, a goal that could accelerate with extraterrestrial partnerships (Musk, 2020).

3.   **Exploration Beyond the Solar System**

- ◦   Alien star maps or navigation technologies could enable missions to nearby star systems like Proxima Centauri, expanding humanity's reach to exoplanets.
- ◦   The Breakthrough Starshot initiative exemplifies humanity's aspirations for interstellar travel, which could gain momentum with extraterrestrial input (Worden et al., 2016).

4. Societal Transformations

1.   **Cultural Renaissance**

- ◦   Access to alien knowledge and art could inspire new cultural movements, redefining human creativity and philosophy.

- The exposure to extraterrestrial worldviews may lead to a deeper appreciation of diversity and interconnectedness.

2.   **Economic Evolution**

- Free energy and advanced technologies could disrupt traditional economic systems, prompting the need for equitable resource distribution.
- A post-scarcity economy might emerge, focused on creativity, collaboration, and exploration rather than survival.

3.   **Global Unity**

- Contact with extraterrestrial civilizations could encourage humanity to transcend national and cultural divisions, fostering a collective identity as cosmic citizens.

5. Ethical and Philosophical Implications

1.   **Responsible Integration of Technologies**

- Humanity must navigate the risks of misusing alien technologies, such as creating weapons or exacerbating inequalities.
- Carl Sagan warned that technological progress without ethical guidance could lead to self-destruction (Sagan, 1994).

2. **Redefining Humanity's Role**

- ○   The shift from an Earth-centric to a universal perspective challenges humanity to reconsider its purpose and responsibilities in the cosmos.
- ○   Philosophers and theologians may explore the implications of becoming part of an intergalactic community.

3. **Cosmic Ethics**

- ○   Collaboration with extraterrestrial civilizations would require the development of ethical frameworks for resource sharing, cultural exchange, and conflict resolution.

6. Insights from Key Figures

1. **Michio Kaku**

- ○   Kaku predicts that extraterrestrial technologies could accelerate humanity's progression to a Type I civilization on the Kardashev Scale, achieving global unity and energy mastery (Kaku, 2018).

2. **Dr. Steven Greer**

○   Greer emphasizes the transformative potential of extraterrestrial technologies, advocating for transparency and public access to these advancements (Greer, 2017).

3.   **Carl Sagan**

○   Sagan envisioned a future where humanity thrives as part of a cosmic community, guided by ethical principles and scientific exploration (Sagan, 1994).

4.   **Freeman Dyson**

○   Dyson's theoretical megastructures highlight the potential for humanity to harness immense energy resources, enabling interstellar exploration (Dyson, 1960).

Looking Ahead

The integration of extraterrestrial technologies and knowledge into human society offers unparalleled opportunities for progress. However, realizing this intergalactic future requires careful planning, ethical foresight, and global collaboration. By embracing the possibilities of a new Golden Age, humanity can redefine its destiny as a species poised to explore and thrive in the cosmos.

Sources

1. Alcubierre, M. (1994). "The Warp Drive: Hyper-Fast Travel Within General Relativity." *Classical and Quantum Gravity*, 11(5), L73–L77.

2. Dyson, F. (1960). "Search for Artificial Stellar Sources of Infrared Radiation." *Science*, 131(3414), 1667–1668.

3. Freitas, R. A. (1999). *Nanomedicine, Volume I: Basic Capabilities*. Landes Bioscience.

4. Greer, S. (2017). *Unacknowledged: An Exposé of the World's Greatest Secret*. A&M Publishing.

5. Kaku, M. (2018). *The Future of Humanity: Terraforming Mars, Interstellar Travel, Immortality, and Our Destiny Beyond Earth*. Doubleday.

6. Musk, E. (2020). *Making Humans a Multiplanetary Species*. SpaceX Presentation.

7. Sagan, C. (1994). *Pale Blue Dot: A Vision of the Human Future in Space*. Random House.

8. Worden, P., et al. (2016). "Breakthrough Starshot: A New Vision for Interstellar Exploration." *Publications of the Astronomical Society of the Pacific*, 128(959).

40

Are We Ready?

> Humanity stands at a crossroads. As we gaze into the stars and consider the possibility of extraterrestrial life, we must ask ourselves: Are we ready to embrace this transformative reality?
> — LG Rice

The journey through this book has explored the scientific, philosophical, historical, and spiritual dimensions of humanity's relationship with extraterrestrial life. As the author, I reflect on the profound implications of alien contact and what it would mean for us as a species. Humanity's readiness to meet this reality depends on our openness, willingness to change, and ability to recognize our shared worthiness to evolve as universal beings.

1. Openness to Possibility

1. **The Vastness of Space**

   ○ The sheer size of the universe makes it improbable that humanity is alone. With billions of galaxies, stars, and planets, the potential for life elsewhere is almost certain.

   ○ Astronomer Carl Sagan once said, "The universe is a pretty big place. If it's just us, seems like an awful waste of space" (Sagan, 1994).

2.　Expanding Human Perspectives

- ° Embracing the possibility of extraterrestrial life requires breaking free from Earth-centric worldviews.
- ° Michio Kaku argues that openness to the unknown is the hallmark of scientific and societal progress, a necessary step toward becoming a Type I civilization (Kaku, 2018).

3.　Breaking the Stigma

- ° The stigma surrounding UFOs and alien encounters hampers serious discussion and research. By fostering open-mindedness, humanity can shift from skepticism to curiosity and exploration.

2. Validating Experiences Across the Globe

1.　Global Consistency in Accounts

- ° Reports of UFOs and alien encounters have been documented across cultures and throughout history. These accounts often share striking similarities, despite arising from unconnected individuals and societies.
- ° Jacques Vallée highlighted that the consistency of these reports suggests a genuine phenomenon that transcends cultural boundaries (Vallée, 1991).

2. **Credible Witnesses and Evidence**

- ○ Military pilots, government officials, and respected scientists have come forward with accounts of encounters, lending credibility to the existence of extraterrestrial phenomena.
- ○ The U.S. government's recent declassification of UAP (unidentified aerial phenomena) data underscores the legitimacy of these observations (ODNI, 2021).

3. **Beyond Coincidence**

- ○ The global nature of these experiences, coupled with physical evidence such as radar tracking and trace materials, makes it implausible to dismiss them as mere coincidences or fabrications.

3. Embracing Change and Progress

1. **Letting Go of Fear**

- ○ Fear of the unknown often hinders progress. Embracing the potential of alien contact requires overcoming fear of change and uncertainty.
- ○ Stephen Hawking warned of potential risks but also emphasized that fear should not prevent humanity from advancing its knowledge and capabilities (Hawking, 2010).

2. **Recognizing Humanity's Worth**

- ° As universal beings, humanity deserves to strive for higher consciousness, peace, love, and harmony. Our evolution is not only a technological journey but also a spiritual one.
- ° Ancient texts and starseed philosophies suggest that humanity's destiny is intertwined with the cosmos, encouraging us to embrace our role as participants in a universal community (Cannon, 1998).

3. **Advancing Together**

- ° Progress requires collaboration across nations, cultures, and disciplines. By uniting as a species, humanity can rise to meet the challenges and opportunities of an interstellar future.

4. My Insights as the Author

Reflecting on the themes explored in this book, I believe:

1. **We Need to Be More Open-Minded**

- ° The vastness of space makes it essential to entertain the possibility of extraterrestrial life. Denying this is not just a rejection of evidence but a failure to embrace the unknown.

2.   **The Evidence is Too Overwhelming to Ignore**

   ○   Accounts of otherworldly experiences from unconnected individuals around the globe cannot be dismissed. These stories, coupled with mounting physical and observational evidence, point to a truth that transcends cultural and geographic boundaries.

3.   **We Should Embrace Change and Progress**

   ○   Humanity's potential is immense. By letting go of fear and embracing our worthiness, we can move toward a higher consciousness rooted in peace, love, and harmony. This is not just a dream but a necessary evolution if we are to join the universal community as responsible and enlightened beings.

5. Are We Ready?

The answer lies in our collective will to embrace the challenges and opportunities that extraterrestrial contact presents. Readiness is not just about technological capability; it is about ethical maturity, global unity, and a willingness to look beyond ourselves.

Humanity stands on the brink of an extraordinary chapter in its history. Whether extraterrestrial contact comes tomorrow or decades from now, our journey as universal beings has already begun. By preparing our minds, hearts, and societies for this reality, we can ensure that the end of isolation leads to the dawn of a new era—one defined by curiosity, collaboration, and cosmic connection.

Sources

1. Cannon, D. (1998). *The Custodians: Beyond Abduction.* Ozark Mountain Publishing.
2. Hawking, S. (2010). *Into the Universe with Stephen Hawking.* Discovery Channel.
3. Kaku, M. (2018). *The Future of Humanity: Terraforming Mars, Interstellar Travel, Immortality, and Our Destiny Beyond Earth.* Doubleday.
4. ODNI (2021). "Preliminary Assessment: Unidentified Aerial Phenomena." Office of the Director of National Intelligence.
5. Sagan, C. (1994). *Pale Blue Dot: A Vision of the Human Future in Space.* Random House.
6. Vallée, J. (1991). *Dimensions: A Casebook of Alien Contact.* Ballantine Books.

Thank You for Reading

Dear Reader,

Thank you for taking the time to explore *What If ETs Are Real?*

I hope this book has sparked your curiosity and provided valuable insights into one of humanity's most profound questions. This journey is far from over, and I encourage you to continue exploring.

Throughout the book, I've cited numerous resources that delve deeper into the topics presented. These are excellent starting points for further research, and I urge you to check them out to expand your understanding and gain even more knowledge about this fascinating subject.

I'd also love to hear your thoughts! Whether you have comments, questions, or simply want to share your perspective, please don't hesitate to reach out. Visit my website at www.authorlgrice.com or email me at hello@authorlgrice.com to join the conversation. Your insights and feedback are invaluable, and I'm always eager to connect with fellow explorers of the unknown.

Thank you again for reading. Here's to curiosity and discovering the infinite possibilities of our universe.

With gratitude,

LG Rice

Visit my website: www.authorlgrice.com
Contact me: hello@authorlgrice.com